Into the Sun

by
Luanne Armstrong

Illustrated by Robin LeDrew

A Hodgepog Book

i

Hodgepog Books acknowledges the ongoing support of the Canada Council for the Arts.

Editors: Luanne Armstrong and Dorothy Woodend

Cover design and inside layout by Linda Uyehara Hoffman
Set in ITC Fenice and ITC Caslon 224 in Quark XPress 4.1
Printed at Hignell Book Printing

A Hodgepog Book for Kids

Published in Canada by Hodgepog Books,
3476 Tupper Street
Vancouver, BC
V5Z 3B7
Telephone (604) 874-1167
Email: dorothy@axion.net

National Library of Canada Cataloguing in Publication Data

Armstrong, Luanne
  Into the sun

  ISBN 0-9686899-9-X

  I. Title.

PS8551.R7638I57   2002   jC813'.54   C2002-910953-1
PZ7.A73375In   2002

The Canada Council | Le Conseil des Arts
for the Arts | du Canada

Thanks hugely for her research, support, and
long friendship, to Robin LeDrew.

Chapter One

"I hate being the oldest," Reine thought to herself. She balanced her three year old sister Pauline, on her lap as the wagon they were all riding in together jolted and banged its way over the rough prairie.

The sun shone down as though it wanted to eat them up. The grass was so tall it brushed against the sides of the wagon. The black pony pulling the wagon struggled along, trying to keep up with the riders on horses surrounding them. Behind their wagon stretched a line of carts, some pulled by oxen, some by horses.

The wheels squeaked and groaned. After a while, the riders pulled ahead and the wagons plodded along. Reine's mother, Marie-Anne, sat at the front of the wagon, holding the reins. Reine's brother, LaPrairie, who was twelve and considered himself almost a man, sat beside her. Next year, Papa had promised him he would have his own horse and be able to ride with the men.

Reine and Pauline, her other brother, Benjamin, who was nine, and her sister Josette, who was only seven, sat in the box of the wagon. The next sister or brother was riding under their mother's bulging apron.

They were all hungry and tired. One of the reasons they were going on this hunt was because they would soon need food for the long winter. Reine's mother had grown a garden, full of cabbage, carrots, onions, turnips, beets, parsnips and potatoes, but they would need more than vegetables to survive the winter.

Even though it was now late summer, they all knew winter would soon be on its way again. They would need a lot of food to survive.

Everyone from their small settlement on the west bank of the Red River had gathered at their log cabin just a few nights ago to discuss what to do. During the long bitterly cold winter, food was crucially important. Reine's father was the best buffalo hunter in the whole community. Every year, he led the fall buffalo hunt which supplied the whole settlement with meat for the winter. The meat they didn't use would be sold to the new people, the Scottish settlers who had come a few years earlier to settle on land that had been bought by Lord Selkirk for them to farm.

When Louis Lagimodiere spoke, the other hunters all listened carefully.

"The buffalo are getting harder to find," he said. "They have changed their migrations. But if the buffalo won't come to us, then we will go to them," he said. "Right now, they are far west and south of the Pembina River. We will be gone a week, maybe ten days. When we come home, we'll have food for the winter."

"I am coming, too," said Reine's mother. "The children and I will come in the wagon."

Louis, Reine's father, sighed. He was used to the independent ways of Marie-Anne, Reine's mother. Marie-Anne and Louis Lagimodiere were famous throughout the western Canadian prairie wilderness. They had traveled in every part of the land while Louis made a living as a trapper and hunter. In her thirteen years, Reine had lived in log cabins, in tipis with friends they had made among the native people, in sod huts, and in flimsy canvas tents. One winter, they even lived in a cave.

Then a few years ago, they had settled among other families on the banks of the Red River in Manitoba. Louis Lagimodiere had worked long and hard to build his family a house, a big house made of logs, the most wonderful place Reine had ever seen.

"All right," he said, "You and the other women will need to organize the wagons and supplies. We will have enough to do getting ready for the hunt."

The other men nodded. There was a lot for everyone to decide. The women clustered together in one corner of the room, talking excitedly. Some decided they would also make the journey. Some of the other women would stay behind to care for the animals. Many of the settlers had managed to get a cow or a few chickens. Last year, somone had arrived with a few pigs. The pigs had been carried in rafts, canoes, and sleds on the long journey which the Scottish settlers had made from York House on Hudson's Bay.

Then each family left. The men would need to look over their guns, their supply of ammunition, saddles, bridles and the care of their sleek swift horses. The women would pack food, blankets, tents, knives and other equipment to get the food ready for winter. There would be so much work to do. The meat would be dried, and mixed with fat and berries to make pemmican. Everyone would be needed to help with the work.

Reine sighed again. She wished she had her own horse to

ride, instead of being stuck in the wagon. She had been riding horses since before she could walk. One of her first memories was riding in front of her mother on the beautiful, gentle pinto mare that was her mother's special pet.

When her brother, Jean Baptiste, was a baby, Reine still rode in front of her mother while the baby rode behind, strapped in a beaded tikanogon. Jean Baptiste had been born unexpectedly, after the beautiful pinto mare, who had been trained to hunt buffalo, ran away with Marie Anne bouncing on her back and baby Reine bouncing in a basket tied to her side. It was a story Reine had heard many times It was why her brother was nicknamed LaPrairie.

When the next baby, Benjamin, was born, her father Louis bought a wagon.

If only she could be riding with the men, Reine thought to herself. Perhaps one day soon, she could have a horse of her own and ride by herself instead of being stuck here in the wagon taking care of all her little brothers and sisters.

They were all hot and restless.

"I'm hungry," whined Pauline.

"Have some water," Reine said.

"Don't want water. Want food," Pauline said sulkily. "I'm hungry, not thirsty."

"We'll have food when we get to camp," Reine said patiently.

"When," Pauline went on stubbornly. "When are we gettin' to camp. When, Reine, when?"

Reine sighed again. Pauline was so stubborn. When she started in on something, she never let it go.

"I'll ask Maman," she said. "Soon."

Up ahead she heard shouts from the men. She stood up in the wagon and peered over her mother's shoulder.

"We are coming to the river," her mother said. "We'll have to be careful when we cross over. Reine, hang on tight to the children."

Her mother was looking very worried.

When they got to the river bank, the men on horseback gathered beside the line of wagons carrying the women and children. They all stared at the river. It was wide, fast and muddy. Reine thought it looked scary and dangerous. None of the smaller children could swim. What if the wagon turned over and they got spilled out into the river?

"Reine, gather the children in your lap and hold on tight," said Maman again. "I am going to drive the horse into the river. The wagon will float. You will be fine. Just hold on tight."

Terrified, Reine gathered Pauline, Josette and Benjamin close to her

Pauline wrapped her arms around Reine's neck in a stranglehold.

"I can't breathe," Reine said, trying to unwrap her arms. Pauline began to whimper.

"Shhhh," Reine said. "We'll be fine. Maman and our brave pony will get us over the river as quick as anything. I know. Let's sing our way over the river."

She began to sing loudly, "En roulant, ma boule roulant, en roulant, ma boule.'

Gradually, the other kids joined in as the wagon lurched

down the bank and into the water. As they got deeper into the river, water came through the floorboards and soaked into their clothes. The cold water was almost a relief after being so long in the hot sun.

Suddenly, the wagon lurched sideways. One side rose high in the air. Reine and her armful of children rolled down to the side of the wagon.

"Hold on," her mother shouted.

Terrified, Reine clutched the side of the wagon with one hand and the children with the other.

She couldn't see anything but she could hear the men shouting, could hear her mother calling. "Help, Louis, help us," her mother shouted.

Then Reine heard her father's strong voice. She struggled to sit up, pushing wet hair out of her eyes. She could hear more splashing, then her father called, "Hold on, hold on, we are going to pull you out. The wagon is stuck in a mudhole." Another black-bearded man appeared on the other side of the wagon with a long coil of rope. Louis and the rest of the men soon had the wagon pulled up on shore.

As soon as they were safe on dry land, all the children piled out of the wagon. Maman started a fire and the children ran to bring armfuls of dry driftwood. Their mother gave them strips of dried meat to toast over the fire and made hot sweet tea to wash it down. All the other wagons had also arrived safely and people began to come to the Lagimodiere fire. Maman handed out cup after cup of tea and slices of bread and meat to each child.

After eating, Reine's mother spread a colourful Hudson's Bay blanket on the sandy bank and lay back in the sun. Pauline curled up beside her. The men squatted around the fire or lay on their backs in the shade of the willow bushes, dozing in the early autumn heat while the women and smaller children curled up on blankets.

Reine and the other children played in the shallow part of the river, splashing each other to cool off. When they were tired of that, they wandered down the bank a little way, exploring and looking for wild crab apples and plums.

"Don't go too far," Reine warned them all. "There might be bears or something. Stay away from the river bank. You might fall in."

In answer, Benjamin started running down the bank.

"Whoopee," he called, "look at me, I'm a wild buffalo, ha ha, you can't catch me, bossy old Reine."

Reine sighed. Of all the children, Benjamin was the hardest to manage because he considered himself too old to be bossed around by her. But he was only nine, too young to be allowed to roam around on his own.

"Come back," she called. "I can hear Maman calling.

Come back." She stood there, wondering which to do, to stay with the other children or run after Ben.

Suddenly she heard a horse behind her. She turned quickly. It was Dan Archibald. He was only fifteen and this was the first year he had been allowed to go on the hunt.

He grinned at her.

"I'll catch him," he said. "Your Maman is calling. We must get going or it will be dark before we camp for the night."

He trotted after Benjamin on his tall brown horse. He looked back and smiled at Reine. His white teeth flashed.

Reine's stomach fluttered. Quickly, she hurried the smaller children back to her mother and then helped to load them in the wagon.

The pony, who had been grazing peacefully on the prairie grass, was backed into the shafts and hitched to the wagon.

"Hup," said Reine's mother quietly. The sturdy black pony dug in his hoofs and pulled the creaking wagon and its heavy load up the river bank and onto the soft prairie grass. Dan came galloping up and dropped the wriggling Benjamin into the wagon.

"Hey, look what I found over there," he laughed. "I think it is a wild bear cub, maybe, or a buffalo calf. It is very strong and likes to fight. I think you should keep an eye on that one."

He laughed again and rode away. Ben sat sulking in the bottom of the wagon.

Reine watched Dan trot away. The sun shone on his black hair. She wished again that she had a horse of her own. Dan's horse was special. Some of the early settlers had brought English horses from back east, tall beautiful creatures. Dan's horse was bred from one of these.

Reine wondered if she could talk her father into getting another horse. Then she could ride beside Dan. Together they could race their horses over the prairie grass. Reine thought how amazed he would be at how well she could ride and how brave she was.

When they finally got to the place where they were going to camp during the hunt, Reine was too busy to think anymore about racing over the prairie. While her father put up their canvas tent, she had to gather dried buffalo manure, which they burned in place of firewood. Then she helped her mother feed the children, get them undressed and washed, braid Josette's and Pauline's long hair and get them settled into the blankets on top of the warm buffalo robes in the tent.

Her father had been busy checking the horses, making sure they were hobbled properly. Her mother was tending the fire, making a large pot of stew and bannock to eat with it. She made the stew with prairie turnips which she had stopped and dug along the journey.

After she had eaten, Reine felt very tired. It had been a long day. She sat on the grass, staring into the golden flames of the fire. This was her favourite time of the day, a time when a faint light in the prairie sky still lingered in the west, when the sounds around her from the distant prairie told of the animals getting ready for the night, some settling in and some waking up.

Reine loved the prairie because it was so full of life. There were the big impressive animals, buffalo, wolves, cougars, bob-cats, but what Reine truly loved were the small creatures, the birds and butterflies, the turtles sunning themselves on the rocks by the river, the little green frogs that sang from the ponds at night, long black garter snakes, hawks which sailed on the wind. She liked to go off by herself and sit quietly while the life of the prairie went on around her. Sometimes she saw amazing things. One dusky evening, she had been sitting quietly by the banks of the Red River. The moon was just rising, full and pearly-white, over the prairie when a flock of geese went by, so huge they almost covered the whole sky. To her they sounded like people talking and murmuring to themselves—the sounds of the wings were like women's skirts brushing over the floor of the sky.

Now as she sat by the fire, she could hear her mother and father talking in low voices inside the tent, probably planning tomorrow's hunt. Tomorrow would be a busy exciting day. Everyone would be working hard—her mother would be helping with the butchering, cutting up the buffalo meat which would hang in the sun and the wind to dry. It was hard, heavy, dirty work. Reine would also be needed to help as much as she could. She would also be needed to look after the smaller children and keep them safe. Wolves and bears often followed the buffalo herds.

A cold lonely wind blew over the prairie, making the tall grass dance and sway. Reine felt cold despite the warmth of the fire. Suddenly, her eye was caught by a long swirl of green and blue light curling across the sky.

"Papa," she called, "the lights, the lights are here."

Papa crawled out of the tent, carrying his big hunting rifle. Other hunters had seen the lights as well.

They began to fire their rifles into the sky, laughing and joking as they fired. Reine knew they did this to drive off any spirits in the sky that might want to ruin the buffalo hunt Gradually, the lights faded and the men put away their rifles.

Reine shivered as the wind blew over the prairie. She was very glad to crawl into bed beside her brothers and sisters and her parents and sleep through the night in their tent under the dancing stars.

Chapter Two

"Let's go, children," Reine called. "We will go fruit picking so Maman will have lots of plums and crab apples with which to make pemmican. Look, I have some bannock and dried fish for a snack. We'll make a fire and cook for ourselves. Come now, our Maman is going to be very busy today."

Obediently, three of them trailed along after her, Pauline holding onto Reine's skirt. Josette held her hand and soon Benjamin ran ahead of them all. LaPrairie had gone with Maman on the wagon to help with the hard work of cutting up the dead buffalo. He had been very proud of himself, especially when Papa gave him one of his old hunting knives for his very own.

Reine sighed. She loved her brothers and sisters but sometimes she really was very tired of looking after them all. She wondered what it would be like to live a different life. Sometimes her mother told stories of growing up in Quebec. It sounded like a lot of fun with lots of other people around, parties, music and dancing.

Somewhere Reine had grandparents she had never seen. All she knew about them came in stories told by her mother and father. Sometimes Reine tried to picture what it would be like to live in a real house, to have a room and a bed of her very own, to be able to go in her room and shut the door.

Since she was born, January 6th, 1807, she had lived in so many places. Reine's mother was always busy cooking, cleaning and caring for their family. Reine loved each new baby that came along and, as she had gotten older, her mother leaned on her more and more to help with the work. Reine sometimes wished, just for a little while, they would all leave her alone.

"Benjamin, stay where I can see you," she called. Sometimes there were bears eating fruit and now was not a good time to be separated.

Instead of slowing down, Benjamin ran faster, disappearing in to the thick tangle of bush ahead of them.

He came running out just as fast.

"There's something in there," he said. "I heard a noise."

"Is it a bear?" Reine said.

"I don't know, I couldn't see. I just heard the bushes crackling."

Reine gathered the children around her, trying to decide what to do. If it was really a bear, they should go back to camp right away. But her mother really needed the fruit. Perhaps Benjamin's imagination had only tricked him, or perhaps he was playing a trick on her.

"Are you sure you saw something?" she asked him.

"Of course I am sure. I think we should go back to camp and get a gun."

"Don't be silly. I can't shoot a gun."

"I can," he said boastfully. "Papa showed me how."

"Wait here," Reine said finally. "All of you stay with Ben. I will go and have a look by myself. If I call to you to run, then run back to camp as fast as you can. Ben, I am putting you in charge."

"I'll go look again, Reine," he offered bravely. But Reine was already sneaking closer and closer to the wall of low tangled trees. They were loaded with wild plums. Her mouth watered. She saw a place where a path wound into the bushes. The branches were interlaced and criss crossed over the path and Reine had to stoop low to get through. Spiderwebs tangled in her hair.

Yuck, she thought, wiping spiderwebs off her face. She hoped the spiders weren't getting in her hair as well.

Suddenly she froze. She heard it too, a rustling sound in the leaves under the bushes. She waited, even though every muscle in her body was screaming at her to run. Then a round brown shape waddled into view. Reine choked with laughter. It was a porcupine, nearsightedly snuffling its way along the ground. Reine stood still and the porcupine went by so close she could have touched it.

She wondered if she should tell her Papa. But if she did, he would kill the porcupine and turn it into dinner. It seemed like such a harmless creature, wandering along on its own. She knew that some of the Indian people often used the quills to decorate their clothes. She squatted down and the porcupine sniffed at her leather moccasins, then waddled away again.

She went to get the children and they all got busy filling their leather bags with plums to take back to the camp.

Soon enough her stomach began to rumble. She heard her mother's voice in the far distance, calling them all back into camp for their noon meal.

She gathered the children, picked up Pauline, who was looking very sleepy, and headed back for camp and their usual lunch of stew and bannock. Only this time, there were also fresh strips of buffalo liver toasting over the fire.

All the men were squatted around her family's fire, while

her mother ladled out stew from her huge iron kettle. Dan Archibald was there, looking very proud of himself. His pants and shirt were spattered with blood.

Reine filled her wooden bowl with stew and a chunk of bannock. She plunked herself down in the long prairie grass to eat, thankful that she could have a few moments to herself. Dan looked across the fire and smiled shyly at her.

She smiled back, then ducked her head behind her hair to hide her red cheeks. She concentrated on finishing her food, then stood up to get herself a cup of tea from the steaming kettle that hung over the fire on an iron tripod.

"Here, let me." Dan was there before her, taking her tin cup from her hand and filling it from the kettle.

When she went to sit down, he followed her and sat beside her on the grass.

"We had a good morning," he said. "There will not be hunger among the people this winter. Your father is a good leader. But I myself killed two buffalo."

"I wish I had my own horse and I could ride whenever I wanted," Reine said wistfully. "It's wonderful, going so fast."

"As long as your horse doesn't step in a hole or fall down in front of a wounded buffalo," he grinned. "Then it is not so wonderful at all."

Reine was silent for a while. Then she said, "I saw a porcupine this morning, while we were picking plums. He came and sniffed my shoe. I was worried in case it was a bear but it was just a silly old porcupine."

"Porcupines aren't silly," he said gently. "My mother says porcupines are the friends of the people. In late winter, when the people are beginning to run short of food, we can always find a porcupine to save us. "

"I didn't want to tell you in case you wanted to eat him," she said.

"I am glad you told me," he said.

"Someday, if you liked, you could go for a ride on my horse," he added.

She stared at him.

"I don't know," she said. "I don't know what my mother would say."

She was feeling confused. Dan was so nice. She knew her mother and father approved of him. She had heard her father talking to one of the other hunters about what a good idea it had been to let Dan come along.

But she wasn't sure how her mother would feel about her going riding with someone like Dan. For one thing, his mother was an Indian woman. It was all very confusing. One of her mother's best friends was an Indian woman. They had been friends for many years and the Indian woman had lived with them for a while and helped to care for the children. Her father also had many friends among the native people. They lived side by side, worked together, hunted together. But she also knew there was a difference between her family and the other people, the Bois-Brulés, as they called themselves, people who were part white, part Indian. Some of the other white people called them half-breeds, and made fun of their way of life which made Reine furious.

But the hardest part was that Reine didn't really know how to make friends. She didn't know any other people her age. She spent all of her time with her family, taking care of the children and helping her mother. Until a few years ago, she and her brothers and sisters were the only white kids she knew. Reine was the second white child born in that part of the Northwest. They were always on the move, as her father hunted and trapped for a living.

Then a few years ago, they settled on the Red River. Because they were French Canadian and Catholic, they weren't really part of the new settlement of Scottish people. But they weren't Bois-Brulés either. Reine knew that everyone liked and respected her father and mother. But much of the time, the Lagimodières stuck to themselves.

Dan seemed to live a much easier life. He seemed to have lots of time to ride his horse, go hunting or be with his friends. She had seen him back at the settlement, riding among a group of friends, all of them laughing and talking at once.

He probably just felt sorry for her, felt her life was dull and boring, he was just being kind to her.

"I must help my mother now," she said, rising to her feet and beginning to gather up cups and bowls.

"I will go to my father's tent," he said. "Tomorrow, if there's time, perhaps you can go for a ride on my horse."

It took Reine a long time to fall asleep that night. Finally, she got up as quietly as she could and went outside to look up at the stars. They were so huge and beautiful; she wondered what they really were. She had asked her father once and he had snorted, "Bright lights in the sky, maybe they are God's candles, eh, little one?" and then he had laughed.

She pictured herself riding swiftly over the prairie, free as the wild buffalo and antelope. She was determined to do it no matter what her mother and father might think.

The next morning came very early. Reine was dimly aware of her father rolling back the blankets and going outside. She opened one eye. Through the open crack of the tent door, she could see a dim grey light. There were faint pink streaks in the eastern sky.

She could hear the thud of horses' hoofs, the crackling from the fire, the low voices of the men as they checked their rifles. She could smell meat toasting on the fire and tea boiling.

Her mother and the other children seemed to be deeply asleep. Reine sat up in bed, slipped on her skirt, her shirt, and her shawl. She tied a scarf over her hair and slipped on her leather moccasins. She waited until the men's voices faded in the distance, then she crept out of the tent and followed them.

It was easy to keep out of sight because of the tall prairie grass which waved its plumey golden tops over her head. The horses had bent down the tall grass, and she could follow these paths. She fell farther and farther behind because the horses were now speeding up. The men's voices stopped and soon she was alone on the prairie.

She could see the sky brightening and long pale pink and orange fingers of light reaching for the sky as the sun began to rise. She hurried as fast as she could. Finally, she came to the top of a small hill and stopped.

Far away, she could see the men on horseback. The horses were running very fast now towards the herd of buffalo. The buffalo were running too. She could hear the first rifle shots. She could tell which rider was her father because of his bright

18

red hat, bobbing like a tiny dot through the clouds of dust around the running buffalo. He was leaning back in his saddle, his rifle propped on the front of the saddle, as he fired at the buffalo, then re-loaded and fired again, all at a full gallop.

But her eyes were looking for the dark brown horse which she knew was carrying Dan Archibald.

Suddenly Reine remembered her mother and the children.

Her mother would have to go help her father. She would be expecting Reine to help with breakfast, with the children. Reine turned and began to run back to the camp. She had to lift up her long skirt, which was by now soaked and heavy with the early morning dew.

When she got back to the camp, her mother was very impatient.

"Reine," she snapped angrily. "Where have you been? I must hurry to help your father. Please feed the children and get them dressed."

Her mother already had the pony hitched to the wagon. She climbed awkwardly into the wagon, while LaPrairie sprang to the seat. She clucked to the pony and then hurried off. The children came out of the tent, yawning and rubbing their eyes. Reine sighed. Why was it always her job to take care of everything?

A pot of barley porridge was bubbling over the fire. Quickly Reine dished it into bowls, one for each child. The porridge was sweetened with maple syrup and dried berries. Reine sighed again. Once in her life she had tasted sugar. It had been at a Christmas party back at the settlement. There had been many strange foods at that party, such as candy, and apples which had been carried in boxes from far away Montreal.

The children ate their porridge and then Reine had to coax them into getting dressed, had to make them line up and stand still while she washed their hands and faces. Then she went to the river to get more water to heat for the dishes.

By the time Reine was done, she was tired and cross. Her feet hurt and her hair needed to be combed and rebraided into the tight braids which she usually wore hanging down her back.

"Benjamin," she called. "Benjamin, I am going to the river to wash. Please watch the children for me."

But her brother was busy. He was sitting astride a log, pretending it was a horse, and shooting pretend buffalo with a long stick. Reine looked around. Her little sisters, Josette and Pauline were playing in the dust with some sticks they were pretending were dolls. They had knotted bits of cloth and hide around the sticks. The camp looked peaceful.

"Ben," she called again. "Ben, did you hear me?" but her nine-year-old brother paid no attention to her at all.

Reine shrugged. Her little brother never did his share of the work. All he did was dream about the day he could have a horse of his own and go hunting like his famous father.

At the river, she carefully washed herself all over with a bit of cloth, then soaked her hair and did it back up in its normal tight braids. She sat very quietly on the sand, watching the life of the river. An eagle soared overhead. As she sat on the sand and followed its flight with her eyes. it circled higher and higher. Reine wondered what the world looked like from so high. Perhaps if the eagle flew high enough, it could see far to the east, to the grandparents she had never seen, far away on the Saguenay River in Quebec; or perhaps it could see far to the south, to the fort at Pembina where she had been born; or to the northwest, to Cumberland House, where her mother and father had gone soon after she was born, just a baby being carried on her mother's back.

Her mother and father loved to tell their children stories

of their adventures. Through the long winter nights, they told stories of their travels over the prairies, of their visits with the Indians and the fur traders, and their encounters with wild animals. Reine wondered about the adventures she would have when she was grown. She would have her own horse, and she would be free to travel wherever and whenever she pleased. She would be the envy of everyone she met. Perhaps she could be an explorer and go to places no one had ever even heard of before.

Suddenly, she heard a terrible scream from the camp. She leapt to her feet. Oh no, she had been daydreaming for too long. Something might have happened to one of the children. She ran as though her feet had wings, all the way back to the camp. When she got there, Benjamin was sitting beside Pauline and Josette. As soon as Pauline saw her, she ran to her and grabbed her skirt.

"Benjamin shot me," Pauline cried. " He said I was a buffalo. I don't want to be a buffalo, Reine."

Reine looked around. She noticed someone had gotten into the food bags and had spilled flour all over the floor of the tent. Reine's heart sank. What a morning she was having.

Angrily, she snatched up the leather food bag. "Who has been spilling food?" she asked. But no one would admit it.

Reine was very busy for the next hour. She swept and cleaned the tent, warmed some water over the fire and washed her brother's and sisters' dirty faces, then warmed some beans and stew for their lunch. After lunch, she sat them in a circle and they played and sang songs together.

Late in the afternoon, she heard the wagon wheels

squawking as the carts returned, carrying their loads of meat and hides. As the wagon creaked to a halt in front of their tents, Reine's mother climbed wearily down off the wagon. The front of her dress and apron was splashed with blood.

She folded her arms across her bulging stomach and sank to the ground. Reine brought her a cup of tea as the children clustered around their weary mother. Then their father thundered up on his big pinto horse. He slid from the saddle and the horse stood still as he dropped the reins to the ground.

Louis Lagimodiere had fulfilled his role as the best buffalo hunter in the Red River settlement.

"Five buffalo I killed, my children," he said. "We will have such a good winter, plenty to eat and our new log house to live in, eh? When we get home, we might have a party in our new house to celebrate. What do you think, my little one," He grabbed Pauline and swung her up in his arms.

They all laughed, caught up in his joyous mood. But their mother soon brought them back to the present.

"We must finish getting this meat cut up and drying in the sun," she said, "Then we will get the fat into our big pot and set it cooking over the fire. We must get the meat made into pemmican as soon as possible. We mustn't waste a single bit after your father worked so hard and risked his life to get it."

Reine heard another horse's hoofs and looked up. It was Dan Archibald, on his big brown horse.

Dan leapt off his horse in a single graceful move. He came over to the fire and squatted down. Reine's mother offered him a cup of tea which he accepted gratefully and drank down in a single gulp.

"It's been a hot thirsty day," he laughed. "But it was also a great day. My father sent me over to invite your family to our tent for supper. My family would like to thank you for your leadership on this hunt, for helping provide us all with food for the winter."

Reine bent her head to hide her face but her mouth curved into a smile anyway. Dan's father was a famous fiddler. Tonight there would be dancing and feasting, storytelling and music, laughter and shared happiness. Perhaps this day, which had been so long and hard, would at least end with a sense of joy and friendship.

"I wondered, sir," Dan went on, "if I can take your horse to the river with mine for a drink. Then I will hobble both of them and turn them loose to rest."

"Thank you, Dan," said Louis. "That would be very kind."

"Perhaps Reine could help me," Dan said quickly. "I know she is good with horses."

Everybody looked at Reine. Reine held her breath.

"Yes," said her mother. "I think that is a good idea. I am sure she would be glad to help you. She works so hard all the time helping her family."

Reine smiled. "Thank you, Maman," she said.

She jumped to her feet and ran and grabbed the reins of her father's big horse. Side by side, she and Dan led the horses to the river. They stripped off the saddles and bridles and blankets.

"Let's give them a bath," Dan said. "They worked very hard today. We owe them a lot."

Reine tucked her long skirt up above her knees and she

and Dan led the horses into the cool water, the horses dipping their heads to snort and sip at the water. They splashed handfuls of water over the horse's sweaty backs and necks, then led them out of the river and let them roll on the soft river sand.

Then they led the tired horses out to where all the other horses were grazing on the rich prairie grass. Reine held each horse while Dan fastened on their hobbles and turned them loose. They waved at one of the men who would stay up all night, guarding the horses and keeping them safe from wolves or thieves.

Then they went back to the river, gathered up the heavy saddles, sweaty blankets, and bridles and took them back to the tents.

"Well, I guess I'll see you later," Dan said smiling. "Do you like to dance?"

"Oh, yes," Reine said. "And I love to listen to the music."

She skipped all the way back to the camp, humming songs to herself .

Chapter Three

The trip back to their settlement near Fort Douglas seemed to take a long time. This time the wagon was full of leather bags of pemmican, and the children had to perch among them like birds. They would all be so glad to get back to their new log house.

Reine curled up in her corner of the squeaking jolting wagon and thought about the past few days. Every day she had worked side by side with her mother, cutting the buffalo meat into thin strips and hanging it in the sun to dry. She also had to cut and gather green willow sticks, buffalo manure and driftwood to keep a fire burning so the smoke would drive away the flies and mosquitoes.

To make pemmican, they filled an enormous Hudson Bay copper kettle with buffalo fat and melted it over a fire. They spread the dried flakes of meat which had been pounded into shreds with a flail onto a buffalo hide. They then dipped out boiling fat from the kettle and poured it over the meat while turning it with a shovel. It took two strong people to make pemmican—one to pour and one to mix. Then they stretched out a buffalo hide and cut it into four pieces. Each piece was made into a bag which held the fresh pemmican. Everyone had helped, even the little children.

They had all been tired from working so hard but in the late afternoon, everone would take a break and gather on the river bank. They would splash in the cool water, while the older boys played and wrestled together on the sand.

The women and smaller children would have naps in the

shade from the tall willow brush. When the sun began to go down and shadows gathered in the pools and hollows of the prairie, all the people would go back to their campfires and have feasts of bannock, buffalo meat and stewed plums and apples. At night they all had gathered together around the fire while Dan's father played the fiddle. Sometimes Reine's mother would tell stories of their many adventures. Other times, the people would sit together and talk and make plans for the coming winter and spring.

When they got home they would have much to do to prepare for the coming winter. Their father Louis would be busy gathering wood for their fireplace to keep them warm. They would have to gather the vegetables from their garden and make a trip to the fort for supplies.

They had lived in their house now for almost two years but it was still amazing to have so much space. Two whole big rooms, one with a clay fireplace at one end, and the other with bunks built around the edges for sleeping. There was even a loft where Maman and Papa slept, with a ladder to climb up and down. Not only that, it even had a cellar, the first house in the Red River settlement to have such a thing. They could store wheat and pemmican in the loft, potatoes, turnips and other food in the cellar.

Outside was a barn where they had a cow, and stalls for their father's saddle horse, and the pony. Reine's mother had even talked about getting some pigs.

Reine was thinking about a new idea. Perhaps she could make one corner of the cabin into a special place, her own place. She had a beautiful new Hudson's Bay blanket for her bunk. Her mother had given her some scraps of cloth to make into a braided rag rug. What she wanted more than anything else was a curtain to hang over her bunk so that she could have some time by herself but she didn't think that would happen. The only way she could get time to herself was to go outside after she had finally done all her chores, lie quietly in the long prairie grass and watch the sky.

At last they arrived at their house. It was wonderful to be home, to be warm and safe all together around the fireplace. For a while, Reine didn't even mind her brothers' noisy wrestling. Benjamin and LaPraire seemed to be always wrestling on the buffalo rug in front of the fire until Maman would lose patience and send them outside. Josette and Pauline pestered Reine for stories, or to make new dolls for them out of scraps of cloth and bits of wood.

Plus Reine had many chores to do. Every day Reine's mother went out to milk the cow. When the milk was cool, she poured the cream off the top of the milk, and Reine's job was to churn the cream into butter which Maman sold at the fort.

Reine's father had gone to Fort Douglas and traded the butter as well as many of their bags of pemmican for wheat and barley which the new settlers were growing. He also brought back a round flat stone called a quern with another round stone for the top. He showed them how to grind the wheat into flour for bread. It was a slow process and took a long time. Benjamin and LaPrairie were supposed to take turns grinding the wheat but usually they started wrestling instead so Maman would send them outside.

"This is how we can make our own flour, my children,"

Papa had boasted. "Next year, we will also grow our own wheat and barley. Our land is rich. What do you think, my children? Your father will not be a hunter or a trapper much longer eh? He will be a farmer instead." He laughed as if this idea was a big joke. Secretly, Reine thought her father would never give up hunting and trapping.

Whenever he told stories of hunting and trapping in the far off northern prairies, his eyes would grow far away. He would always end by saying "Those were great days, eh, Marie. Days of adventure!" Marie-Anne always nodded and smiled but Reine knew her mother was very glad to be living in the new house and not in a tipi or a tent.

The busy days flew by and one day when Reine got up and went outside the ground was carpeted with a blanket of white.

"Snow," she announced to her family. "The snow is here at last." They all went outside to have a look at the bright new land, carpeted in white. Although their house had windows, the windows were covered in buffalo hide. Even though it was scraped thin and clean to let in the light, they couldn't see through it.

Reine's chores kept her busy, but whenever she had a spare moment, she found herself dreaming about Dan. She missed his company, his easy laugh and bright blue eyes but it was more than that. She wasn't sure what to do about this new feeling, but she was sure she didn't want anyone else to know about it. She was sure Dan also had lots of work to do, helping his father and mother care for their family but she couldn't help but wonder if he ever thought about her, as well.

After the first snow, it seemed to go on snowing day after

day. Gradually, the family tramped deep trails between the barn and the house, and the woodshed and the house. There was also a long path to the water hole at the river, which they had to chop open every morning to fetch water for washing and cooking. Twice every day they led the horses and cow down to the river for a drink.

It got colder and colder. It was so cold that the snow squeaked underfoot and the air bit into their lungs and cheeks and noses when they went outside. Reine wrapped herself in shawls and put extra straw in her moccasins but still she came inside from her expeditions to the river feeling like she might never get warm again.

Then one day, a man trudged through the deep snow on showshoes, and came in without knocking. It was Mr. Archibald, Dan's father.

"Just come to see how you folks are doing," he said, sitting down by the fireplace and accepting a cup of tea. "Brought you a bag of salt."

Reine was glad. Salt was hard to get. The native people made salt from some hot salty springs in the north near Lake Winnipeg.

Mr. Archibald and Louis Lagimodiere drank cup after cup of tea. Then they both lit their pipes and sat smoking and staring into the fire. Reine sat cross-legged on the floor near the fireplace, listening to the men. She liked to listen to their stories of hunting, trapping, seeing wild animals and traveling. She was also busy learning to knit. Her mother had recently managed to trade for some wool from the few sheep at Fort Douglas.

Reine's mother had been so excited. "Now we will have new warm socks and hats and scarves for everyone," she said.

"Lots of snow," Mr. Archibald said. He puffed on his pipe. "Should be good for the crops."

"I am going to plant wheat and barley this year," said Louis.

"As long as there are no grasshoppers. I remember five years ago, when the grasshoppers were hatching out of the ground, it looked like the ground was boiling," said Mr. Archibald. "Then they ate every speck of grass and wheat. Those were hard hungry years," he added.

"If it hadn't been for the help of the Indians, feeding people and taking them into their tents for the winter, many people would have starved," Louis said. "Yes, we have had more than enough trouble for the last little while, grasshoppers, starvation, along with people fighting each other, quarreling over whether we should all be hunters or trappers or farmers. What does it matter?"

"We need to find ways to live together peacefully and help each other." Reine's mother said from her corner, where she was mixing bread dough.

"Might be a different kind of trouble this year," Mr. Archibald said. "My wife's people are saying when spring comes and all this snow melts, we should be prepared to move to higher ground. They've seen it before. They say the river will come here and eat our houses like so many sticks of wood. They are worried for us all."

Reine's parents looked at each other.

"Mr. Archibald," Reine's mother said. "I have lived all

over this wild country. I chose to follow my husband and live the life he had chosen for us. My children and I have lived in tents and tipis and sod huts. Now for the first time we are snug and at home in our own house. We are so happy here."

"This is a strong house and I built it on high ground," Louis added. "I don't believe the river can ever come this high. But if it does, my family and I will be prepared. We will do whatever we have to to save our home. "

"I believe we must stay here and make our farms and homes here," Marie said. "This is a good place, good land, a place to raise our children."

"Well," Mr. Archibald said, "we will have to wait and see what the warm weather brings."

Reine wanted to ask Mr. Archibald how Dan was doing but she didn't dare. She helped her mother get supper on the table and then listened while the adults exchanged news from the fort and the surrounding community.

"We've got to keep an eye on each other. It's important to know whether anyone is short of food, whether anyone is sick or needs medicine. There is one family, the Menzies, down the river from you with a new baby that needs some milk. They've been feeding it fish gruel but it is still ailing. I knew your family had a milk cow and might be able to help out."

"Of course," Reine's mother said. "I will go there tomorrow."

"It's a hard trip in all this deep snow," Mr. Archibald warned. "Be sure to dress up warm. It can get mighty cold."

After supper, everyone went to bed. Mr. Archibald rolled himself in a blanket and slept on the buffalo skin rug in front of the warm fireplace. In the morning, when Reine woke the children, he had already gotten up and gone on his way.

In the late afternoon, Reine sat on her bunk in the corner, wrapped in a shawl. Her busy fingers flew. She had finished knitting her first pair of wool socks. Next, she thought, she would make herself a hat and dye it bright red with some of the red ochre dye her mother had traded for from the Indians.

Chapter Four

One night when Reine and all her brothers and sisters were sound asleep, they were awakened by someone banging hard on their door. Reine heard her father get up and answer the door.

"Oh no," he said, "I'll come right away." He shrugged on his heavy buffalo skin coat and his big leather boots and left the house.

Reine wrapped her shawl around her shoulders and slipped out of bed. Her mother was up too, adding wood to the fire, pouring water in the kettle and hanging it over the fire.

"What is going on, Maman?" Reine said.

"A terrible thing," she said. "A fire at the Archibalds' house. All of the men have gone to help. Mrs. Archibald and her children will be coming here. We must find some extra blankets and make places for them to sleep. And we must have food and tea ready. They will so scared and cold and upset."

Reine helped her mother make some bannock and a big pot of rubadoo, made with fried potatoes, onions and pemmican. Soon they heard voices, then feet stomping off snow outside their door.

Reine's mother opened the door and Mrs. Archibald and her three younger children came in. Reine's mother showed them where to sit by the fire to keep warm and then served them the food. Reine handed them warm cups of tea, then hovered nearby, wanting to do more to help and trying to figure out how she could ask about Dan. She knew he had stayed behind with the other men to help fight the fire.

Mrs. Archibald had long black hair in tight braids. She had a heavy shawl wrapped around her shoulders. Her frightened children gathered close to her and she made room for the two youngest to crawl into her lap. They stared around the room with big dark eyes. Reine smiled at them and they smiled shyly back.

"We are so sorry for your misfortune," said Reine's mother. "But of course, we will all do what we can to help out. Tomorrow, people will bring food and blankets, pots and pans. You can stay here as long as you wish until your house is rebuilt."

"When the weather gets better, we will go to the camp of my own people," Mrs. Archibald said. "But right now it is too cold and there is too much snow for these little ones." She looked very sad. She was rocking back and forth on the chair as she held her children close.

"You mustn't worry about anything more," Reine's mother said. "You have had a terrible scare. Right now, we will get you and the children settled here by the fire where you will be warm. The men probably won't come back until morning and they will be cold and hungry. We must all try to get some rest. Tomorrow we will decide what needs to be done."

Mrs.Archibald nodded wearily. "You are a good kind friend," she said. "We will always remember your friendship."

Reine helped her mother lay buffalo robes and blankets on the floor by the fire. Mrs. Archibald lay down and gathered her children close to her. Reine went back to her bunk and lay down but she couldn't sleep. She wished there was a window in their cabin so she could look out and see the men approaching. Her father had promised to make two real glass windows in the spring. He might be able to get glass at the fort, brought at great expense all the way from Montreal. He would have to trade many beaver and other skins for them.

Finally Reine dozed off but woke again when she heard voices coming toward the cabin. Even before her mother could get up, she sprang out of bed and ran to fill the kettle and hang it over the fire.

She heard more feet stamping and men's loud voices. She heard horses calling back and forth. The men were putting the horses away in the barn. Then the door opened and suddenly their small house seemed to be full of men, tall men in buffalo skin coats which shed snow onto the floor where it melted in small puddles. Reine's father was welcoming everyone—Mr. Archibald was there with Dan, both of them looking very tired. Their faces were smudged with black soot. Two other men came in as well—Reine knew they had cabins just to the north, a man named John Robertson and another named Pierre Couteau.

"I am so sorry, Madam," said Reine's father to Mrs. Archibald, who had gotten to her feet, leaving her children sleeping. "We saved everything we could and put it all in one of the storage sheds. We were able to save most of your food and clothes, some blankets and furniture, but your house is gone, I'm afraid. As soon as we can get everyone together, we will come help you to rebuild."

"Thank you so much for your help," said Mrs. Archibald. She moved to stand beside her husband and he folded her in his arms. They stood there a long moment with their arms around each other, rocking back and forth a little.

Reine smiled at Dan who smiled back but neither of them said anything. Reine moved to the fire where the water was now boiling for tea. She made the tea and served it out to all the tired men. Her mother, in the meantime, was busy making more food, cooking more pemmican, potatoes and bannock, putting on beans to boil for a later meal at midday.

Reine suddenly felt very tired but she had much to do before she could rest. She could hear her younger brothers and sisters stirring. Soon they would be up, asking questions, needing to be washed, dressed and fed.

"Reine," said her mother. "Please take the buckets and go to the river for water."

Reine nodded. She went and wrapped herself in her heaviest shawl, then slipped thick, straw-filled, leather moccasins on her feet. The river wasn't far but the very last part was down a steep bank. She would have to carry the buckets and an axe to chop through the ice which would have formed on the hole overnight.

Once outside, she blinked her eyes against the dawn light on the white snow. She stood a moment on the top of the hill, looking around. She could see the smoke from several distant houses rising into the air. The world was white and still under the bright sun. She slipped the wooden yoke for carrying the heavy buckets onto her shoulders.

In a few months, she knew the prairie would be buzzing with life, new grass poking up through the ground, geese, swans, and pelicans on the river, rabbits and gophers hiding in the grass. One sign the children always watched for was the garter snakes coming out of the ground. There was a place nearby where the snakes hibernated in huge round balls over the winter. When they emerged at last, everyone knew for sure that the long cold was over. The other sight Reine loved more than anything was the purple crocus, which bloomed in such numbers that it covered the prairie in purple silk.

Then Reine thought about what Mr. Archibald had said about the river flooding in the spring. She tried to picture the reddish-brown water rising as far as their house and failed. The river was far below, buried under its winter coat of thick white snow. It seemed far away, trapped and lifeless, and nothing she had to worry about right now.

When she came back in the house, Mrs. Archibald smiled at her. She spoke to Reine in the Cree language, which Reine understood a little. She smiled and answered back in the few Cree words she knew.

That evening, when all the other children were in bed, Mrs. Archibald beckoned to Reine. She showed her the piece of leather she was decorating with beads, dyed porcupine quills and round pieces of hollow bone.

After that, Reine took time to sit with Mrs. Archibald every day. She practiced speaking Cree, and learned how to decorate leather clothing with patterns of beads and dyed quills. Mrs. Archibald was famous in the Red River settlement for her wonderful beadwork. She seemed to enjoy talking to Reine in bits of the Cree language, or sometimes in Cree and French mixed together. Whenever Reine sat down beside her, Mrs. Archibald would show her how to make whatever new pattern she was creating. Together, she and Reine made a pair of beautiful new beaded moccasins for Reine to wear on special occasions.

Chapter Five

The Archibalds stayed for two long weeks and after a while, despite their best intentions, they all started to get on each other's nerves. It still snowed every day. Reine's maman made her take all the children out each afternoon to play. They made holes and caves in the snow, and paths so they could play fox and geese.

When the Archibalds finally left, the cabin seemed big and almost quiet. But by now, Reine and her brothers and sisters were so tired of the snow. They were all looking forward to spring when the snow would be gone and they could run in their bare feet over the green prairie.

Reine's papa got up early every morning and went off to help Mr. Archibald build their new cabin. Reine's maman was tired and slow with the weight of the baby she was carrying inside her, and she sat down often during the day, sighing and holding her hand to her side.

Reine now went outside every morning to milk the cow and feed their few chickens. She hauled water from the river twice a day. Often, when she went to haul water, she spent some time on the riverbank staring at the bright sky or exploring the willow thickets that fringed the river. She saw many interesting things. There were usually deer and antelope browsing on the willow thickets. Once she even saw an enormous moose which crashed away through the brush as soon as it caught a glimpse of Reine's red headscarf.

Sometimes when she stood on the river bank, she thought about Dan Archibald and his family. The little cabin had been crowded to overflowing but somehow they had all managed to get along despite their occasional irritation. Reine had tried to think of extra games like Cat's Cradle, and songs to keep the little children amused and in the evenings, Mr. Archibald had played to them on his fiddle while they danced and sang.

Often Dan helped Reine to care for the children. Together, they would sit on the buffalo skin rug in front of the fireplace and tell stories or sing old French-Canadian or Scottish songs. Sometimes they would talk about the things they loved to do in the summer, playing on the river, or riding horses, or exploring the trails over the prairie.

Dan would also go with Reine to help milk the cow, or carry the heavy water buckets up from the river. Now, she missed his company, his jokes and his teasing. He could always make her laugh.

Some days now, she was surprised to find herself feeling lonely despite the constant company of her brothers and sisters. Then she would curl up on her bunk and work at her knitting, or her sewing. She was beginning to be able to sew well enough to help her mother with the endless ongoing chore of making clothing, knitting socks, scarves and hats, and piecing together quilts to keep them all warm. There was always so much to do.

The most peaceful times in the small cabin were in the evenings, when they all gathered in front of the fire. Then Reine's father and mother would tell them stories of the family's early days, when the family traveled all over the west, hunting and fur trapping.

One night, Louis said, "Children, did I ever tell you about

the time your mother got lost in the forest when she was growing up, back in Maskinonge?"

"No, no," they all cried. "Tell us!"

Actually, they had heard the story many times before but
they loved to hear their father's stories over and over.

"Your mother was always so adventurous," their father
said. "From an early age, I was always hearing stories about
her in the small town of Maskinonge. People used to wonder
what would happen to such a little girl who used to have so
many adventures. Well, now they know, she got married and
moved far far away." He laughed and paused to fill his pipe.
Then he gazed into the fire for a long time.

"What happened, Papa?" LaPrairie said impatiently. "Tell
us the story."

"She was just a little girl, only ten years old, when she
went out with the other village children to pick raspberries.
They went farther and farther into the woods and soon it was
getting dark and time to go home. But then everyone said,
where is Marie-Anne Gaboury? What has happened to Marie-
Anne? They called and called but there was no answer. Finally, they had to go away, because it was getting dark and they
were afraid there would be wild animals. They had to go and
tell Marie-Anne's parents that their little girl was lost in the
deep forest.

But the next morning, Monsieur Gaboury went out to get
wood to light his fire and there was his daughter, Marie-Anne,
running towards him. She had spent the whole night in the
forest all alone and then come home by herself in the morning.
When they asked her what had happened, she said she saw

some Indians and so she ran and hid. Then it got dark and she couldn't find her way home. In the morning, she was so lucky. She wandered through the forest until she found the river and then she could find her way home. Just imagine, children, if she had stayed lost, none of you would be here and I would be all alone and lonely."

They were silent, contemplating such a terrible idea. Then their father laughed again.

"Come now, don't be sad," he said. "I will tell you another happier story about your beautiful mother. You see, when she was a young girl, she was the prettiest woman in the village. All the young men wanted to dance with her at the community dances. I was always away hunting and trapping so I never thought I had any chance with her. When I went to a dance, I didn't want to fight my way through the crowd of young men around your mother. So I stayed away. But then at one dance, I looked up and to my astonishment, who should I see coming towards me but Marie-Anne Gaboury. She asked me to dance. I was so amazed you could have knocked me down with a feather. But of course I said yes. Oh, she was so beautiful. And she still is," he said.

Their mother laughed. "Your father was always trying to get away," she said, "but I surprised him. When we got married, he thought he would go off hunting and trapping without me but I fooled him. I came with him and we are still having our adventures, now all of us together."

Reine felt very proud of her family. She knew her mother and father worked very hard to keep them all fed and warm through the long cold winter. She was glad she was part of such a strong family. That night when she went to bed, she thought about her mother lost in the dark forest. She was so glad they were all together and safe in their little log house.

The next morning, after breakfast, their father had a surprise for them.

"Okay, everyone," said Louis Lagimodiere. "Reine, help your brothers and sisters get on their winter clothes. We are going tobogganing."

How could they do that, Reine thought. They didn't have a toboggan. All they had was an old sleigh that their pony pulled over the snow.

"Hurrah," shouted LaPrairie and Benjamin together. They ran to pull on thick woolen socks, heavy winter moccasins, coats, the mitts and hats that Maman and Reine had knitted. Reine got herself and the two little girls dressed and they all went outside into the bright sunshine. It was a relief to be outside after the darkness of the small cabin.

"Come with me, everyone," their father said. He led them into the barn and uncovered a bundle from some hay in the corner. It was a toboggan made of long curved bones, the ribs from buffalo that had been smoothed and polished. The ribs were tied together with strips of shaganappi, or rawhide.

"Mr. Archibald brought it over," he said. "He and his family wanted to say thank you for our hospitality. Now with this toboggan we can fly like the wind over the snow."

Their father led them to the top of a hill sloping down to the river. The toboggan was only long enough for a couple of them to sit on. Their father sat at the front and the little children sat in the middle. Reine waited at the top of the hill. The

snow was packed hard and frozen on top. The sled flew down the hill like the wind but it was a long hard trudge back up to the top. After two trips, the two little girls were tired and Reine took them back to the house but LaPrairie, Benjamin, and their father continued sliding, shouting and laughing as they flew down the hill again and again.

Reine curled up on her bunk. She was thinking about Dan again. She had an idea. She was thinking about writing him a letter. It would be difficult. The family only had a few pieces of paper, one pen and one bottle of ink. Their mother had given them all a few lessons through the long dark winter days and Reine knew how to write, just a little. But she never wrote anything—who would she write to? And there was nothing to read. So writing a letter would be a big adventure. What would she say? How would she say it?

She slid off the bunk and went to her mother who was busy kneading bread dough.

"Mama, can I have a piece of paper?"

Her mother looked at her. "Hmm," she said, "now why would my little Reine be wanting a piece of paper. Is there a special someone she might be wanting to send a letter to?"

Reine felt her face grow warm. "I just want to practice my writing," she said. "Maybe sometime I could write a letter to Grandme're and Granpapa Gaboury, back in Maskinonge."

"Now that is a wonderful idea," said Reine's mother. "I try to write them a letter every year, and they try to write to me. But it is such a long way and the letters take a long time to come and go. They have to go by canoe. I worry so much that something will happen to my Maman or Papa and I won't even know. Oh, it has been so long since I was young and carefree in Maskinonge." Reine's mother's face turned sad. She took the lump of dough, shaped it into two long loaves, placed them carefully into pans, covered the pans with a clean cloth and placed the two pans near the fireplace for the bread dough to rise.

"I was so young and happy the day your father and I got married. When we left to come out to the west, I never thought about how I was leaving my family and I might never see them again. Then I was so busy learning to be a wife and a mother, meeting new people, learning the ways of the prairie, that I didn't think about it very much. But now some days I miss my mother and father so much. But it would be too far to travel to go see them. For now, letters will have to do."

Suddenly, she sat down on a chair and clutched her side. "My goodness," she said, "your new brother or sister wants some attention, I think. Reine, perhaps you should go and get your father."

Reine was startled by the look on her mother's face. She ran and threw her shawl over her shoulders. Then she slipped on her heavy winter moccasins and ran out the door.

Her father was trudging towards the cabin through the snow with her two brothers behind him on the toboggan.

"Papa, papa," she called. "Please come, Maman is asking for you."

"Boys," he said, "put the toboggan away in the barn. Reine, go and hitch the pony to the cart. For tonight, you and the other children can go sleep with the Beauprés."

In the house, Reine helped get the children ready to leave. Her father would take them to the neighbours, and then he would have to ride fast as the wind to the camp of Chief Peguis and bring back an Indian woman elder to help with the baby. Her mother had a lot of last minute chores for them all to do, setting the bread to rise, packing food to take with them, and taking care of the animals.

After the door closed behind them, Reine and the other children got in the sleigh and their father covered them with warm buffalo robes. Then he climbed up on the sleigh and clucked to the black pony. Reine wrapped her arms around Pauline and Josette, who snuggled into her for warmth. LaPrairie and Benjamin sat on either side of the cart.

Reine felt tears come to her eyes. She hoped her Maman would be okay. Reine wished she could have stayed home, to help take care of her.

"Reine," said Pauline. "Is our Maman going to be okay?"

Reine looked up. All her brothers and sisters were looking at her with big scared eyes. Reine hugged them closer.

"We must be brave and strong," she said, "like our Maman and Papa. We will be back home soon with our new baby brother or sister. So come now, we will sing a song for each other."

They sang their favourite song, "En roulant, ma boule roulant," and soon they had arrived at the cabin of Monsieur and Madame Beauprés. Monsieur Beauprés was a tall man with a long black beard and his wife Madame Beauprés was short and round. They came out of their cabin to welcome the Lagimodiere children.

When they went inside, Reine noticed that their cabin was much smaller and didn't have bunks around the sides. Instead, there was a sleeping loft with a ladder to climb up with. Madame and Monsieur Beauprés, unlike most of their other neighbours, had no children. They seemed very pleased to see the Lagimodiere children.

"Come in, come in," boomed Monsieur Beauprés. "Come and get warm." Soon they were all settled around the fireplace. Their father kissed them all good-bye then left and the children drank tea to get warm. Madame Beauprés served them all bannock covered with rich maple syrup and soon they were feeling more relaxed although Pauline stayed in Reine's lap and Josette kept her hand tucked into Reine's hand. The children weren't used to being in someone else's home. They weren't quite sure how to behave.

The Beauprés didn't seem too sure about having so many children in their home either.

"It is very cold, eh?" said Monsieur Beauprés. "Lots of snow."

"Yes, sir," Reine agreed politely.

"Your father tells me he will be planting wheat this spring," he added.

"I think so," said Reine.

"Humph!" said Monsieur Beauprés. "This is a country for hunters, trappers, fur traders, brave men. What will happen when the good prairie grass is all plowed under? Where will the buffalo go then? What will we fur traders do?" He glared at Reine as if it was all her fault.

Reine wriggled uncomfortably. "My father says there is room for everyone," she said.

"Farming will be the ruin of this country," he exclaimed.

"Albert," intervened Madame Beauprés. "Don't badger the children. Come, my dears, I will show you where you can sleep. You can spread out the buffalo robes and blankets you brought with you."

50

51

Reine and the other children were glad to crawl up the ladder to the loft and into the sleeping robes.

"Reine," said LaPrairie, when they were all in bed. "Do you think Monsieur Beauprés is angry at Papa?"

"No, no," said Reine. "I think he is a good man. He is just worried, perhaps. Shall I tell you a story to put you to sleep?"

"Yes, please," they all chorused.

"This happened when LaPrairie and I were just babies, before the rest of you were born," said Reine. "We were living in the northwest, far from here, and LaPrairie was just a little baby. Maman says she used to carry us in baskets, one on either side of her pony. One day, one of the Indian chiefs came to her. He wanted to adopt LaPrairie for his own little boy. Maman says he brought her his best buffalo horse, then one by one, he brought her all the rest of his horses. But she just laughed and shook her head. She tried to explain to him in Cree that she would never give one of us away. Finally, she said, he went away, very sad because he wanted to adopt LaPrairie so bad."

They were all silent after this.

"I would have been a great Cree warrior," LaPrairie boasted softly. "I would have been a hunter, with my own horse."

"But you wouldn't have been with Maman and Papa," Reine pointed out. "You wouldn't have been part of our family."

"Maybe when I am older, I can go visit those people," he said. "Maybe we could all go."

"Can we go home in the morning?" Josette asked.

"Papa will come to get us as soon as Maman is better," Reine said. "Everything will be fine. I just know it will."

Chapter Six

When their father brought them home the next day, they all crowded in the house to stare at their new baby brother. Maman was sitting in a chair beside the fire. The baby was small, red and very sleepy. He opened his blue eyes, looked around, waved his tiny fists, then went back to sleep.

"His name is Romain," Maman said. "Here, Reine, why don't you hold him for me while I make us all some supper."

Reine held the baby very carefully. Then each of the other children wanted a turn holding him until it was time to eat and Maman put him to sleep in a woven basket cradle which was tied to the rafters. It was easy for Maman to reach out a hand and set the cradle rocking if Romain was fretful.

After the excitement of the baby died down, they went back to their old routines, but the world outside was slowly changing. It had stopped snowing and was getting warmer. During the day, puddles formed in the paths between the snow banks. Then they froze again at night and the children could slide on them when they came outside in the morning. The ice also made walking tricky. Reine had to be very careful with the heavy water buckets. Her moccasins slipped and slid on the icy surface, and several times she fell and had to go back to the house in wet clothes.

Then, gradually, spring came to the Red River Valley! Although there was still snow in some places, green shoots of grass were poking through the muddy ground. The air was full of bird song—ducks and geese were settling into the ponds and sloughs all in backwaters beside the river, while other birds rocked and sang from every bush and branch. At night a loud chorus of frogs sang from the river banks.

One late afternoon, when everyone else was doing something—Maman was taking a nap with their new baby brother cuddled beside her, the younger children had gone off with Papa to visit their new neighbours, the boys had been set to work by Papa cleaning out the barn, a smelly dusty job that Reine was very glad she didn't have to do—suddenly, for a change, there was nothing for her to do. She crept outside, expecting every minute for someone's voice to call her back but no one did.

Outside, she began skipping and humming to herself. The sun was warm on her face. Her long braids swung down her back and her long skirts swung around her legs. The land behind the cabin was very flat and she had to make her way through the tufts of long dead grass, like thick wool, that covered the ground. She noticed a purple crocus poking through the grass, just beginning to open. She knelt down. The cup of the crocus was like a beautiful shiny purple bowl, with a golden centre. It looked like a golden eye, turned upwards into the sun's gaze. As she watched, a bumblebee fumbled its way inside the crocus. She touched her finger to the satin side of the flower in a secret loving greeting.

Far at the back of their land was a ridge, and at the top of the ridge, there was a long strip of sand, with a high rock sticking up out of the sand like a sentinel. Reine slipped off her moccasins and began to dance, enjoying the feel of her bare feet on the warm and slippery sand. She bowed to her imaginary partner, picked her skirt up in her hands and waltzed around in a circle, humming. She wished that Dan Archibald was there to dance with her. She curtseyed to an imaginary Dan, held out her hand and whirled off round and round.

When she stopped whirling and stood still, the prairie seemed suddenly very silent. She realized her feet were cold and sore. She slipped her moccasins back on and climbed to the top of the sentinel rock. A lonely wind whipped strands of hair in her face. She stood up, turned and faced west, turned her face into the sun. Far over to the west was where she had been born, where she had traveled so many miles with her family. This was her land now, where she belonged, where she would always belong. Even though it had been a new place for her mother and father, it wasn't a new place for her. It was the place she knew best, the only place she wanted to be. She hoped nothing would ever happen to change that.

The wind was getting stronger and stronger. She began to shiver. It was time to go back to the warm cabin. Her mother might be awake by now and would be needing help with the baby while she made supper for all of them. She turned around and looked at the ice-covered river below. She knew that under the ice, the water was running fierce and fast. It was a battle between the ice and the river. Each day, the sun thinned the ice a little but it still kept the river locked in its icy jail.

She knew that her father was worried about the river. Every day, he went and looked at the brownish gray water that ran between the riverbank and the ice. Every day, when Reine took the heavy buckets to fill with water for cooking and washing and cleaning, more and more of the path she usually followed was swallowed up by the water. She knew this happened every year and she wondered why Papa was so worried. She always thought it was very exciting, the swell of the brown freezing water, roaring past. Reine thought the river had a voice—or maybe it was many voices. Some days she stood and listened to the river, thinking if she listened hard and long enough she might actually hear something she could understand. Some days the river sounded like a whole crowd of people all talking together at once. Other days, the river sounded like it had one voice, a deep gravelly thundery voice, rather like her Papa's when he was angry.

The next day was so warm that even Maman came outside with the new baby and sat on the steps of the cabin, enjoying the sun. Reine and her brothers and sisters ran round and round in their bare feet on the grass. The cow and her new baby calf came and looked over the fence. The two horses caught the spirit of play and ran round and round their pasture, kicking up their heels and pretending to be fierce wild horses.

"Look, look," LaPrairie called. He and Benjamin had found a nest of baby rabbits. They all went to have a look. The baby rabbits crouched very still and even let the children pick them up. But Maman said, "Don't disturb them. Their mother is probably nearby, worrying about her babies. Someday we might need them for our dinner so let us leave them to grow up in peace."

That night, it was so warm in the cabin that Reine could barely sleep. Even though Papa had let the fire in the big fireplace go out for the first time in months, Reine was still hot. She tossed and turned. From far away, she could hear the growling of the river. It sounded louder than usual. She sat up in bed, worrying. Perhaps she should go out and have a look at the river. Perhaps it had gotten angry overnight and was coming to eat up their small cabin. Then she heard her father get up. She heard the squeak from the leather hinges on the heavy front door. She heaved a sigh and relaxed. Her papa was always on the alert, looking after them. He was the bravest, strongest hunter in the settlement. He would make sure no harm came to their family.

Reine curled up in her bunk and began to tell herself a story. She often did this to put herself to sleep. She imagined herself and Dan Archibald riding over the green prairie, through endless waves of tall grass. They were on their way to rescue someone—perhaps a family in need of food or medicine. Their horses were tall and strong—the sky was a clear blue. Reine imagined herself on the back of her swift strong horse and, to the rhythm of its rocking gallop, she fell asleep.

The next day, the sun shone hot and sharp over the prairie. That morning, as they were eating their porridge, they heard a strange crackling, roaring noise. "The ice," Papa, roared, "there she goes."

They all went running outside. Sure enough, the last of the ice in the river had broken up. It was floating in huge blocks and chunks on the grey tossing water. The water was singing with a new loud voice. Chunks of ice were tossed into the air, rolled over, and ground together into splinters. They all stared at it with wide eyes.

"Come children, finish your breakfast. Today we have much to do," Maman finally reminded them.

Maman had decided this year, they would have an even bigger garden where they could grow enough turnips and potatoes to be able to share with all their neighbours. Every year, Maman wrapped precious packets of seeds and put them on shelves in the cabin. She had also saved a bag of potatoes to plant for this year. They all laughed when Maman brought out the bag. Spindly white potato tendrils waved in every direction —the poor potatoes seemed to be reaching blindly for the warmth and light of the sun. Maman cut the potatoes into small chunks and then gave each child a bag of potato chunks to plant in the ground which Papa had plowed up.

This year she was trying some new seeds, watermelon seeds that she had gotten from a trader at Fort Douglas. Reine couldn't imagine what a watermelon might look or taste like. Her mother also had some apple seeds which she planted in a row beside the garden fence.

"Just imagine, my children," she said. "Someday we will have our own apple trees growing in our garden."

Papa had borrowed a team of big black oxen from the Archibalds. Dan had brought the oxen over one morning, spent the day plowing, and then had stayed for dinner and overnight.

Reine and the other children had admired the gentle strong oxen. The oxen had long sharp horns, so the children were all afraid at first to go to close, but when they saw how gentle the oxen were and how easily Dan handled them, they lost their fear. Dan had even encouraged Reine to take a turn at plowing with the oxen. He had shown her how to hold the handles of the plow, how to command the oxen with her voice,

Hup, to make them go, *gee* or *haw* to make them turn, and *whoa* to make them stop. It was very hard to keep the oxen going in a straight line, as well as to hold the plow so the point dug into the ground. Reine gave up very quickly but she and Dan laughed and giggled over her attempts.

That night they had a special dinner. Papa had been fishing. He had caught many whitefish, trout and perch. Maman had fried them with onions and potatoes, and there was a pudding made from dried plums for dessert.

Dan and Papa had talked about buffalo hunting and where they might go on a spring hunt. Reine felt a tingle of excitement when she heard that. She loved camping and visiting with their neighbours. It was so exciting for everyone. And it would be wonderful to have fresh meat.

They talked about the Archibalds' new house. After they finished their own spring plowing, Dan's mother and father were planning to have a dance to celebrate finishing their house

After supper, Dan got on his hands and knees and pretended to be a wild horse while the smaller children took turns sliding off his back. Then they sat by the fire just before bedtime while Maman made them a special treat. She brought out the very last of jug of maple syrup which had been made from sap tapped from maple trees near the Red River and they ate it poured over warm fresh bread.

Then they curled in their bunks and went to sleep. In the morning, Dan left right after breakfast. Papa went and harnessed the oxen and spent the rest of the day plowing. Maman and all the children raked the ground in the garden smooth and helped plant the seeds that would supply them with food for the next long winter.

A week later Dan came back to fetch the oxen.

"We have finished putting our seeds in the ground," he said. "My father sends word that you are all welcome to our house tomorrow night for a dance. There will be food, music, and celebration."

He stayed for only a little while then hitched up the oxen to his family's old wooden cart and drove away. There was so much work to do. Reine knew that. Still she wished he had stayed just a little bit longer.

That afternoon, they carried water from the river to water their new garden. It was hot heavy work, carrying bucket after bucket up the long hill. When they were done, Reine went to sit on her bunk and drew the curtain for privacy. She lit a candle for light. She was cross and tired. She had torn the hem of her skirt that afternoon when she tripped and fell. Not only was the skirt torn, it was also muddy and damp. Reine only had one other skirt but that was pretty ragged as well. She wished she had something pretty to wear to the dance, something new, something she hadn't worn a thousand times already, even a bright red ribbon to tie in her hair.

After a while, she got down the little folded packet of beads that Mrs. Archibald had given her, and began to make two beaded rosettes to tie in her long hair.

"Reine, Reine, where are you?" her mother called. For once, Reine didn't answer. She wanted to finish her beadwork.

Then her mother yanked the curtain aside.

"Reine, I need you to help me," she said. "Didn't you hear

me calling?"

Reine sighed. "Coming, Maman," she said, and sat up, but very slowly. Then she stood up, also very slowly. She walked across the floor towards her mother, shuffling her feet.

"Your new baby brother just doesn't want to sleep," Maman said. "I need you to rock him while I make a pot of beans for the supper tomorrow night."

Beans, Reine thought. Why do we always have to eat beans and more beans? She knew that they were short of food, until her Papa and the other men could go hunting and until the new plants came up in the garden.

It was the hungry time of the year, just when everything was turning green and beautiful outside, they and the other settlers were running short of food. Oh well, there would be lots of food at the dance, even if much of it was the same, beans, bannock, jerky, pemmican, boiled potatoes and turnips, and maybe, if they were lucky, and someone still had some sugar or maple syrup, some pies or cakes.

Reine sat in the rocking chair with Romain, who whimpered and nuzzled Reine's shoulder. Reine rocked and rocked, changing the baby's position, but nothing helped. The baby still fretted, fussed and whimpered. Finally the whimpering turned into a full bellow.

"Reine, what are you doing?" her mother snapped.

"It's not my fault," Reine snapped back. "This stupid baby won't go to sleep."

"Reine, never say that about your own flesh and blood," her mother said. "Your family is more important than anything else. Never be rude to them. What is the matter with everyone today? Everyone is so cranky and irritable. Go outside and help your father then if you are going to be mean to the baby."

Now Reine felt really terrible. How could she have been so rude to her mother? She wandered outside, scuffing her bare feet on the rough wooden floor.

Outside, she stopped. The sky was a funny colour, a kind of dull flat yellow. A harsh wind was whipping and tearing over the prairie, tugging at the grass, whistling through the willow brush, yanking at the laundry which Reine's mother had hung on a line that morning.

Even while Reine was watching, a rag blew off the line and went bouncing and tearing over the ground. Reine ran after it, grabbed it, then ran to the line and began pulling the clothes off the line as fast as she could. When she had them all gathered in her arms, she went back into the cabins.

"Maman," she gasped. "There's a terrible wind. I think a storm is coming. I can't see Papa and the other children."

Reine's mother went to the door, squinting into the yellow light.

"Where can they be?" she said. "My poor little ones. Reine, look after the baby, I am going out to look for your father."

Reine's mother threw a shawl over her shoulders and rushed out the door. Reine checked on the baby, who was now sleeping peacefully. She finished folding the clothes and began to put them away on the shelves at the back of the cabin. Outside, she heard a loud crack of thunder.

Anxiously, she went and looked out the door. The sky was

now a dark purple. While Reine watched, lightning streaked out of the sky towards the prairie, followed by the rumble and crash of thunder. It began to rain, gently at first, then harder and harder. Reine heard crashing and banging on the roof of the cabin and she realized the rain had turned to hail. Large round chunks of ice were falling out of the sky and bouncing all over the roof, the yard, the chicken house and the barn. The horses and the cow headed into the barn for shelter, the chickens had already hidden themselves in their chicken house.

Where were her mother and father and the other children? Frantic now, Reine tried to peer through the fuzzy curtain of rain and hail, hoping they were all right. The baby began to cry and Reine closed the door, went back into the cabin, picked up the baby, sat in the rocking chair and rocked and sang. The baby went back to sleep in Reine's arms, while outside the thunder and wind and rain and hail sounded like a herd of stampeding buffalo. When the hail stopped pounding on the roof, Reine put the baby down and went to the door again.

There they were, her maman and papa, each one leading a child by the hand. LaPrairie and Benjamin were running ahead. They were laughing and splashing through the puddles and piles of ice left by the storm.

"Reine," her mother called, when they all got close to the cabin. "We had to hide under a tree to get away from the hail. Oh, it was frightening. Are you all right? Is the baby all right?"

"He woke up but I sang him to sleep," said Reine. Her bad temper had gone. She was so glad to see her family safe and sound, she could have hugged and kissed them all.

They all went into the cabin together, shaking out their wet clothes, talking about their narrow escape and the size of the hailstones. The rain had now settled into a steady drum on the roof. Far away, Reine could still hear grumbles of thunder.

That night, after everyone had settled into their bunks, and Maman and Papa were sitting in front of the fire, Reine got up again.

"Maman," she said hesitantly.

"Yes, my dear one." her mother said. "Come and sit with me the way you used to do. I remember when you were a baby, I would sit and rock you in front of the fire wherever we were living and sing you the songs I learned growing up on the Maskinonge."

Her mother moved over and Reine snuggled into the tiny leftover space in the rocking chair.

"Maman," Reine said in a tiny voice. "Today I tore my skirt."

"Yes," said her mother, still rocking. "I saw."

"My other skirt is thin and ragged."

"Yes," her mother said, and sighed. "We must get you some new clothes. One of the settlers across the river may be setting up a loom to weave cloth. And we can get some more wool to knit you a new shawl. When the harvest comes in this fall, we will trade at the fort for some cloth. All of you will need winter clothes, extra thick moccasins and socks, hats, jackets. I am glad you are learning to sew and knit, my Reine. You are such a help to me."

"Maman," said Reine, a little desperately, "What about the party tomorrow?"

"Yes," said her mother, "it should be a fine party. There are many new people who have come to our community and we will finally all get a chance to meet. Even our new priest, the good Father Gaboury, will be there. I hope there is a chance to talk about building a church. The Scottish settlers have their church but we need our own Catholic church."

"Maman," Reine said. "I am not going. I have nothing to wear."

"Nothing to wear?" repeated her mother. "Of course, you have clothes to wear. We will mend your skirt, that won't take long."

"Maman," said Reine, "I want a new skirt."

"A new skirt? Wherever will we get a new skirt?"

"I don't know." Reine said. She hung her head down. Her lip trembled.

"A new skirt," her mother repeated thoughtfully. "Hmm, yes, there will be dancing tomorrow, all the community will be there. Perhaps the governor will come. You are fourteen now. Yes, perhaps you are right. Perhaps it is time for a new skirt. Go to bed, my Reine. Let me think about this. Let me see what I can do."

In the morning, when Reine woke up and came yawning to the fire for breakfast, her mother smiled.

"If we all work hard today, I think I have solved the mystery of your new skirt. Look what I remembered. "

Her mother lifted a folded skirt off the bench seat by the wooden table.

"You are growing so tall, my beautiful daughter, that I think this will fit you."

It was a long skirt made of dark blue velvety material.

"It was mine," said Marie Lagimodiere, "when I was young and beautiful. I have been saving it for years. It has gone all over these wild prairies with me, But now it is just the right size for you. Then with a nice white blouse and your red shawl, and two red ribbons to tie back your hair, you will be so beautiful. Remember, you were named for the King."

Maman had named her Reine because her birthday was also the birthday of King George the Third, the English king who lived far over the ocean but somehow ruled over them all.

"Thank you, Maman, thank you," Reine said, and ran to hide the precious new skirt in her bunk. All day Reine worked with a light heart but all day, as well, she listened as the rain pounded on the roof and the wind whistled past their door.

By late afternoon, they were ready to go. Papa had harnessed the pony to the cart—they wrapped themselves well in shawls and blankets, then they all piled into the cart. Papa pulled a buffalo robe rug over them.

"Stay underneath," he ordered, "or you will look like drowned baby beavers when you get to the party."

It was stuffy and dark under the buffalo robe and the wind kept blowing the rain in sideways anyway, but at least they weren't drenched and soaking wet when they arrived at the Archibald house. There were several wagons in the yard. The horses or oxen pulling them had been unhitched and put in the barn out of the rain.

While Papa went to put their pony away, Reine, Maman and the other children ran for the house.

The inside of the log cabin blazed with light from candles

66

set high on the new log walls. There were benches around the edges of the room and at one end of the room, long tables were covered with platters and bowls of food. The women and children gathered at one end of the room, and the men at the other.

In the middle of the room, Mr. Archibald and two other men were tuning their homemade fiddles. One man had an accordion—another had a tin whistle. The sounds they were making were so strange that Reine clapped her hands over her ears. She looked around to see who else had arrived.

"Reine, help me unwrap the children and hang their cloaks near the fireplace to dry." said Maman, and Reine hurried to help her mother. Other people were coming in the door as well—the room was filling quickly. There was a buzz of laughter, chatter, greetings being called back and forth in French, English, Gaelic, Cree and a mixture of all four.

Reine found places on one of the benches for the children to sit, then she had time to look around again. She saw Dan Archibald in the corner of the room but he was talking to a group of young men. Reine turned her head away and smoothed down her beautiful blue skirt. She had worn a red shawl over her shoulders and her long blond hair was braided smooth and tied with two red ribbons. She wore the beaded medallions in her hair. Around her waist she had an embroidered red sash, and on her feet, the new moccasins with many coloured beads.

"LaPrairie, sit still," she snapped. "Benjamin, don't pull Josette's hair."

Oh, sometimes it was hard to have so many brothers and

sisters. Maman was talking to several of the other women as they laid out even more platters of food. Reine sat and listened to the voices around her. The cabin was a babble of many voices speaking. Then Reine heard a familiar voice emerge above the others.

Papa was surrounded by a group of men. Reine could overhear enough of what they were saying to know they were continuing to make plans to go hunting very soon.

"As soon as this rain lets up," she heard Papa saying. " We all need fresh meat and Governor McDonnell has assured me they will buy all the buffalo meat, pemmican and hides we can supply. We are all running short of food. The new settlers depend on us."

"Every year, the buffalo get harder to find," grumbled one of the men. "They are moving off farther to the west. We will have to send out scouts to find the main herd."

"There is still a lot of snow to the northwest," said another man, a tall Cree man with long braids. "My scouts have been out looking for the buffalo, but there is too much snow. Deep snow. Hard to get through."

"We need the meat," said Papa. "We have no choice. We have women and children to care for. In the meantime, while we are waiting for the snow to melt, we will go shooting ducks and pigeons. We should put some nets in the river for fish. There is always plenty of food in this land if we want to go after it."

Their voices got lower as they moved away to make plans for hunting and fishing. Now one of the fiddle players had finished tuning his fiddle and stood up. He started to play a tune, a quick dancing tune, and soon the other two players joined in. People stood and listened at first, then one couple after another moved to the centre of the floor as everyone else moved to the sides to make room.

People began dancing, weaving in and out in an intricate pattern of steps, whirling around, bowing and changing places. Some of the dances were the Red River Jig, the Double Jig, Strip the Willow, Rabbit Chase, Tucker Circle, Drops of Brandy. The Red River Jig was everyone's favourite, because it was the liveliest.

They also danced the rabbit chase dance. The men and women stood in a row, their partners opposite them. One couple danced up and down within the column and parted at the end of it. The woman went behind the women's column and the man behind the men's. When they got half way up the column, they stopped and the man chased his partner in and out of the column until he caught her. Then they would start over and the woman would do the chasing.

During the handkerchief dance, a man got up with a handkerchief in his hand, tied it around a girl or woman's neck, danced with her and then kissed her. Then the girl got up, danced around the hall behind her partner, chose another man, tied the handkerchief around his neck and kissed him. And so it went until every man and woman had been kissed.

Reine was eager to dance but instead she sat very quietly and studied the pattern of beads on her beautiful new moccasins that Mrs. Archibald had helped her to make.

"Hello," said a voice near her ear. Reine looked up, startled. Dan Archibald was looking down at the floor, frowning.

"Is there a hole in the floor and the Red River coming through?" he asked.

"Pardon?" said Reine.

"You were staring at the floor so hard, I thought something important must be happening to it." Dan laughed.

"I was thinking," Reine said.

"Yes?"

"I was thinking about my Maman and Papa. They work so hard, perhaps sometimes I am not the best daughter. Sometimes I am rude and ungrateful."

Dan laughed. "You work hard too," he said. "I have seen you. I have so much respect for your Papa and Maman. You have a wonderful family. And I have come to invite you to a special event. Next week, there is a dance in the camp of my mother's people to celebrate my cousin's wedding. There will be a feast. I wondered if you would like to come?"

Reine felt her face burning. A whole day and night with Dan, without her family? It seemed a strange idea, but also exciting.

"I will have to ask my Maman and Papa," she said hesitantly.

"Well, let's go ask them then," he said. Reine looked at him admiringly. Dan was so brave.

They made their way across the floor to where Papa was standing with the other men.

"Monsieur Lagimodiere," said Dan. "I was wondering if Mademoiselle Reine would be allowed to come with our family to celebrate my cousin's wedding. We will be gone one day and one night. I can bring over an extra horse for her."

But before Papa could answer, LaPrairie who had followed them, said excitedly, "Can I go too, Dan?"

"Maybe," Dan said.

They all looked at Papa. "Hmm," he said. "I will have to talk to Maman."

They waited while he went across the floor to the women's side, pulled Maman aside and talked to her.

He came back smiling. "I am sure your family will take good care of Reine and LaPrairie," he said. "You have our permission."

Dan turned and bowed low to Reine. "Miss Reine Lagimodiere, would you dance with me?"

Reine reached out her hand. Dan took it and led her into the middle of the floor, where they soon joined the other couples whirling around to the music of the fiddles.

Oh, how she loved dancing, Reine thought, as her feet wove quick intricate patterns in time to the music. The fringes on her beautiful shawl also leapt and danced. The cabin was a whirling mass of colour and light and sound. Reine caught Dan's eye. He grinned at her and she smiled back.

Chapter Seven

As they came over the hill, Reine could see the Cree camp in the hollow of the valley below. The tipis were so beautiful, tall, white, and painted with amazing designs. As they rode towards the camp, children and dogs came running to meet them. Other people came out of the tipis and from around the campfire. Soon they were surrounded by laughing, smiling people greeting Dan, his mother and father, his two little sisters and his baby brother.

They all dismounted and the horses were led away. They followed Dan's mother into a large tipi. Mrs. Archibald was laughing and crying at once, hugging and talking to a whole crowd of people. There were so many people coming and going that Reine's head was whirling. Eventually, they were all settled around the fire, sitting on soft buffalo robes and blankets, everyone talking very fast.

Soon bowls of food were handed around, roast duck, chunks of fish, buffalo stew, pemmican, and bannock. A kettle of tea simmered over the fire. Reine looked around in wonder.

Suddenly a young woman sat down beside her. "Hallo," she said in a mixture of Cree and broken English. "I am Dan's special friend also."

The two young women stared at each other. The Cree girl had beautiful long black hair tied in braids. She was wearing a beaded leather dress, with a cape on the back decorated with a fringe of feathers. She had some faint blue tattoos on her face. Reine thought she was very beautiful.

"My name is Pippicho. And you are Reine? Dan has told

me about you. He says you are a very hard worker, very good girl. So, you have known Dan a long time?" she went on. "He and I have been playing together since we were little children." She giggled. "He comes here to visit me sometimes."

Reine couldn't think of a single thing to say. Finally she said, "I met him a couple of years ago. He comes hunting with my father."

"Oh yes, he is a very good hunter, very strong," said the young Cree woman. Then she rose. "I will see you later at the dancing." She left the tipi and Reine stared after her.

Reine looked across the fire to where Dan and LaPrairie were sitting with the men. Her face was hot. Why had he invited her here to this celebration if he already had a special friend here? How was she going to ignore him enough to get through the evening and the long ride home tomorrow?

After they had eaten, they all moved outside to a clear place where a large circle of grass had been beaten down. Reine sat quietly, enthralled in spite of herself at the singing, the drumming, the dancing. Pippicho came out with a group of other beautiful young women and danced. But after they finished dancing, they stood giggling together, talking behind their hands and staring at Reine. She tried to ignore them but her face burned.

Then came a group of young men dressed in wonderful bird costumes. Each one imitated a particular kind of bird. It was such a beautiful dance that Reine almost forgot her embarrasment.

LaPrairie had obviously found some friends to play with. She saw him occasionally, running in and out of the firelight, playing with a whole group of other young boys. When it was their turn to dance, he danced with them, looking very serious, imitating the steps as best he could.

Finally, there was a dance in which everyone, including the visitors, were invited to join. Hesitantly, Reine stood up and began to step around in the circle.

"How do you like my family?" Dan's voice said in her ear.

"They're very nice," Reine said stiffly.

"I saw that you met my cousin," he went on cheerfully.

"Yes, I certainly did." Reine lifted her chin high in the air and danced a little faster to get ahead of Dan.

"She is very nice, my cousin," Dan said, dancing a little faster to keep up.

"Yes, I am sure she is," Reine said. She wanted to run out of the circle of dancers, find a place to sit that was quiet and dark, but she knew that would be considered very rude.

"She thinks she wants to marry me but I don't want to marry anyone, just yet. I want to travel, have adventures, visit my northern relatives."

"That's nice," Reine said. "I think I have to go sit down now. I am feeling very tired."

She walked away to the side of the circle and flopped onto the grass. When Mrs. Archibald came over to ask what was the matter, she repeated that she was very tired.

"Oh you poor little one," said Mrs. Archibald. "Come, I will show you where you can sleep."

But sleep didn't come easily to Reine that night.

In the morning, she rose early, feeling groggy, drank tea with Mrs. Archibald, then helped her get the children ready for the trip back to the settlement. Dan kept giving her puzzled looks but she ignored him.

When they were finally on their horses, and when the last good-bye had been called and the barking dogs and shouting children were out of sight, she urged her horse ahead of the rest.

But Dan's horse soon caught up with hers.

"Do you feel all right?" he asked. "My mother thinks you are needing one of her special herb teas. She is very good at making herb teas." He laughed but Reine didn't laugh with him.

"I am fine, thank you," she said. "I don't need any tea. Perhaps you could take some to your cousin."

"My cousin," he echoed in astonishment.

Then his eyebrows shot up in comic amusement. "Oh, my cousin. What did she say to you?"

"She said she was your special friend," Reine said. Her cheeks were burning again. She wished she could jump off her horse and hide herself in a gopher hole.

"She is my childhood friend and my cousin," he said. "Our mothers are sisters. That makes her special. But that is all."

"Oh," said Reine. Now she felt even more foolish.

"You know," said Dan, "there is a place just past here that is flat and good for racing. Do you think your horse could beat mine?"

"Of course," she said. "Just watch me."

She dug in her heels and soon the two horses were flying over the flat prairie. The wind whipped Reine's hair into her eyes and mouth. She laughed out loud for sheer pleasure. Suddenly Dan's horse began to pass hers. She leaned low over her horse's neck, dug in her heels, and urged it on. Side by side, she and Dan pounded along together until they were forced to pull up by a patch of brush and trees.

They were both laughing now.

Chapter Eight

Reine slept in late the next morning. The rain had finally stopped and the warm sun had come out. The prairie was steaming itself dry under the sun.

Reine grabbed a piece of hot bannock from the pan by the fireplace and ran out into the sun. She had so much to think about.

Memories of the last few days whirled through her head—first, memories of the dance. It had been such an amazing time. They had all danced and danced and then later, they gathered around the fiddlers and sang song after song. At midnight, they all gathered around the tables and ate their fill. There were many wonderful kinds of food, some of which Reine had never tasted before. There was roast pork and wild rice, fish rolls, sturgeon steaks, fried fish, rubadoo and corn pudding. For dessert, there was plum pudding with maple syrup, dried apple pie, even two huge cakes. Someone had made birch syrup from tapping the birch trees that grew up and down the river. It tasted almost the same as maple syrup.

Then she thought about her evening at the Cree camp. It had been much the same except the food, the music and the language was different. But it was still people being together and having a wonderful celebration.

She yawned. She felt so tired. This morning, Papa had gotten up very early and left when the first light of dawn was showing over the prairie. He and the other men were heading off on a hunt for pigeons, geese and ducks. Mmm, Reine thought. Roast duck. That would be such a treat.

And Papa had also said he would soon take them all fishing. He had brought home a boat, a wonderful boat, a wooden dugout made of a single huge log. It even had oars with which to paddle. He had taken them for a row and showed them how to use it, but the river was too rough and fast even for the huge strength of Papa.

"Soon," he said, "when our beautiful Red River is quiet again, I will take you all for a ride in the boat."

Reine could still hear the fiddle music playing in her head. She gathered the hem of her old torn ragged skirt in her hands and began to skip and jig over the rough prairie grass.

"Reine," her mother's voice called. "Where are you?"

Reine stopped dancing and went back in the house. Her mother was stirring the oatmeal over the fire.

"The young ones need to have breakfast and get washed and dressed. Your little brother Romain is so cranky this morning."

"I heard Papa leaving this morning," Reine said, as she gathered up Pauline and Josette and began to comb and braid their long hair. Then she poured a pan of warm water, lined all the children up and washed their hands and faces, one by one. The boys squirmed and made terrible faces when she poked in their ears with the washcloth, but she made them stand still until she was done.

"Okay now, time to eat," she said and they gathered around the table set with bowls of oatmeal and warm cream fresh from their milk cow.

After they had finished eating, Reine got them all dressed while her mother nursed cranky young Romain. When that was finally done, they all went out to play in the sunshine.

"Let's play fox and geese," Reine said, and they began playing and hiding in the many trails made in the grass and brush around their cabin.

"Reine, I am going to harness the pony," Maman called. "I have promised to visit Madame Paquin. Her youngest baby is so ill. She is terribly worried. It's her first little one. I told her I would bring her some of our good fresh milk. I will take Romain and leave the other children with you. I don't know how long I will be."

Her mother was looking tired and worried.

"We will be fine, Maman," Reine said.

"There is bread and fish and cold potatoes for your lunch. Oh dear, mon petit," she said, as Romain let out a fresh wail. Maman jiggled him in her arms.

"He is extra hungry from all that dancing, I think," Maman said. "Here, Reine, you will have to hold him while I go and harness the pony."

While Maman was at the barn, Reine danced around through the grass with Romain, bouncing him extra hard whenever he started to wail and by the time Maman came back, he was quiet, and drifting off to sleep. She took him in the cabin to lay him down.

"Oh thank you Reine," Maman cried. "You are so good with the children. You are such a good daughter. And now I must go."

She wrapped her grey shawl around herself, layering the baby in its folds, then swept out the door. Reine could hear her call good-bye, then she heard the clop-clopping of the pony's hoofs, the squeaking of the wagon wheels as it pulled away from their farm.

The cabin felt cold and lonesome without Maman's warm presence inside it. She decided to work on her sewing. She would sit outside in the sun. That way she could keep an eye on LaPrairie, Josette, Benjamin and Pauline at the same time.

She worked in the sun until she felt sleepy, then she went inside to get lunch ready. Suddenly, she heard LaPrairie calling her. It didn't sound like his normal voice—he sounded frightened.

"Reine," he said, poking his face inside the open cabin door. "Come quick. Something is happening. I don't understand. It's the river."

Reine ran out of the cabin and followed her brother down the slope to the river. The river was a strange muddy grey colour. Instead of rushing by the way it usually did, it seemed to have slowed. Its voice had changed—it was whispering, hissing, rumbling. It seemed to have a million new voices.

A few days earlier, when the ice had broken up all over the river and the river had run free in the sparkling sun, it had been so exciting and beautiful. But now the river felt strange, menacing. There were still huge chunks of grey ice racing in the current, some rearing up like frightened horses.

But the river was behaving very strangely.

"The river is rising, look at it."

All the children stood together in a frightened clump, staring at the river. While they watched, it was creeping up the bank, slowly, but fast enough that they could actually see it rise. A line of foam, ice and sticks marked its edge.

"What is going on?" Reine said. "I don't understand. How can it be rising so fast?"

"What are we going to do, Reine?" said Josette.

"I don't know," she said. Reine's mind was whirling. Nothing like this had ever happened before. But both Maman and Papa were away and it was up to her to protect their home, her brothers and sisters, their animals.

"We'll just keep an eye on it," she said finally. "I don't understand what is going on but it is not dangerous yet."

She picked up a stick, walked up the bank, and drove it with all her might into the sandy soil.

"There, we can watch this stick from the house and see if the water rises past it. Perhaps it is only rising from all the rain last night and it will soon stop. Right now, we are going to eat our lunch. We will sit outside where we can watch the river. If it keeps rising, we'll make a bundle of food and clothing and head for the Paquins' house, where Maman is."

Quietly, they all trailed behind her up the hill to the house. They got their food and sat outside on the ground. At the end of an hour, the river was almost to the stick.

Grimly, Reine marched down the hill, pulled the stick out of the ground and stuck it back in again farther up.

Then she went in the house and began packing things. First, she got one of the large baskets that Maman used to carry things. It had leather straps, made of shaganappi. It could hang off a saddle or be fastened to the side of a wagon. Once this basket had carried Reine hanging from the saddle of her mother's horse.

In the basket she put some pemmican, a sack of flour, a

sack of beans, some potatoes and the last of their turnips. On top of the food, she put some clothes, and a blanket. Then she got down another basket and filled it with more clothing and blankets.

For a moment, she stopped, running her fingers around the smooth top of the basket. This basket was a gift from Chief Peguis, after they had lived with his family for a winter.

She had been only eight that winter they spent in the tent of Chief Peguis of the Saulteaux people. He was one of Maman and Papa's best friends, although they hadn't seen him for a while. He didn't like to come into the settlement.

But Reine had loved living in the tipi. At night, she curled close to Maman's side, her and LaPrairie, Josette, Benjamin and Pauline, the new baby. They slept on warm fur robes, with more fur robes piled over them. The tipi was warm and light in the middle near the fire, but dark and cold at the edges. There were always people coming and going, always food cooking over the fire, people sitting around, telling stories or singing.

Chief Peguis always used to beckon her to come sit by his side during the long evenings. He loved her long blond hair and blue eyes, her mother said. After a while, she began to understand what people were saying to her. She had felt so safe there.

Maman had told them they were staying there because Papa had gone away on a long journey. He had carried some messages for Lord Selkirk to the far, far away place called Montreal. Reine had tried to imagine how far it must be, or what it might look like but she couldn't. Her mother told her that there were many houses and many other white people but then Reine had almost never seen a real house and very few white people, so in her mind, what she imagined was a prairie covered with many many tall tipis.

She knew Maman was worried about Papa. Once she overheard some trappers talking to Chief Peguis about some men who wanted to hurt her dear Papa. She was very frightened but her mother told her not to worry. Her father was the greatest hunter and trapper in the Northwest. He was very brave and strong. He would be fine.

And then one day, there he was, stooping to come in the door of the tipi, bending over to gather them all in his big strong arms, his clothes smelling of the forest and far away places. On his side was strapped a long bright sword, a gift from Lord Selkirk for his bravery.

After that, they lived many more places, traveling all over until Papa built them their big new log house. The sword hung over the fireplace where everyone who came in admired it.

And now they had been living in their beautiful log house for almost three years. Surely the river wouldn't come and eat up all their hard work, their garden, the barn, the chickens, the plowed field sown with wheat to be harvested in the fall and made into flour and bread.

Maman had been so happy the day this house had been finished.

"At last," she said, over and over, "a real house. A real table. Even real beds. Even windows. "

Maman had walked around and around the house, looking at everything and exclaiming over it. Then she had unpacked the heavy flatiron she had brought with her all the way from Quebec and which she had carried with her all over the prairies.

"Now even my iron has a home," she laughed.

Sighing, Reine now fetched the iron down from its shelf over the fireplace and put it in the basket. Then she put in the heavy kettle and the big black cast iron frying pan. When she was finished, the baskets were very heavy.

LaPrairie came inside. "We have to take Papa's sword," he said.

"It's too heavy," Reine argued. "And it won't fit in the basket."

"I will carry it," LaPrairie said. "This sword is important, Reine."

Reine frowned, thought for a moment. "You're right," she said. "But you will have to take care of it."

Carefully, LaPrairie strapped the sword so it hung down his back and they both went back outside.

"It's still rising," LaPrairie said. "I wish Papa was here. If it comes up much farther, I am going to let the cow out of the pen and chase her up the hill."

"What are we going to do if Papa and Maman don't come?" said Benjamin. "What if the river keeps rising?"

"Where can we go, Reine?" said Pauline. "I want Maman to come home right now."

Reine looked at them all. She looked at LaPrairie. He was almost as old as she. He was so much like Papa, hard working, strong, quiet.

She looked back at the river. It was now past the second post she had put in the ground.

She looked around. What a strange afternoon. The sky was blue, birds wheeled and sang above them; everything was normal except for this creeping menace, this grey line of dirty water with a froth of white bubbles at the edge, with sticks and weeds and a swirl of driftwood. Willow bushes now waved their green feathered tips wildly above the surging water. Out in the middle of the rushing water, she could see broken trees being carried along by the river.

The water was now up to the top of the bank that led down to the river. From there, the land that led back to their house and barn was flat. Even as she watched, little fingers of water crept forward among the grass. It was as if the river had grown suddenly into some mysterious monster—it made everything seem unreal, as if the land they were standing on, the house, the familiar line of prairie and sky, might dissolve and turn into some other mysterious thing before their very eyes.

"What are you going to do, Reine?" asked Josette. She slipped her small hand into Reine's hand and looked up at her big sister. Always before, Reine had been able to take care of things. That was why her mother leaned on her and trusted her.

"You are so strong, Reine, so dependable," her mother always said. But now, when her family needed her the most, she couldn't think, couldn't gather her scattered thoughts together, couldn't figure out what needed to be done to combat this creeping menace.

"I don't know," Reine said. "Let me think!"

"We have to go to the neighbours, to the Paquin's to find Maman," she said finally. "We need help."

The Lagimodieres were not used to asking for help. They were the family others turned to. They were the family that always had extra food or extra clothing. Louis Lagimodiere was the leader of the hunt, the man the other settlers depended on for food. The women came to Marie Lagimodiere to learn how to grow a garden in this new land. They came for advice when their children got sick or when they were due to have a child.

But now there was nothing Reine could think to do. They needed help. She had to get her brothers and sisters to safety.

"LaPrairie, open the pasture gate so the cow can get free. Open the chicken house so the chickens can escape. Children, we are going to head south, to the neighbours. We will take the baskets of food with us."

"But what about Papa? When he comes home, he will find us gone," cried Benjamin. "I want to stay here. I want Maman and Papa."

"Me too," cried Josette.

Little Pauline said nothing, only pressed close to Reine's side, her eyes, large and round, fixed on the advancing water.

"It is not safe here," Reine said. "LaPrairie, you and Benjamin carry the baskets. Pauline and Josette, hold my hands."

The little group of children began to walk south along the river, heading for the nearest neighbours. But they hadn't gone very far when they realized they had run into a problem.

Papa had built their house on a flat piece of land near the place where the Seine River ran into the Red River.

"This is rich land," he had told them, "land which will grow wheat and cattle and fine horses. Someday, my children, there will be beautiful farms here, big houses, a town with a church and a school. My hunting and trapping days will be over. One day your Papa will become a rich farmer, eh, what do you think about that?"

Their land ran back from the river for almost a mile. Most of it was flat, except for the small hill with the pointed rock on top that Reine loved to climb. On the north side of their property was the Seine River. But on the south was a gully which had a creek running in it in the spring but was dry the rest of the year. But now the gully was full of a raging torrent of muddy gray brown water.

"Back," said Reine, we'll have to go back from the river, towards the prairie. We'll try and go around the ravine."

They turned around and headed towards the back of their property. In some places, they had to struggle through thickets of brush and willow. They were getting tired and hot and LaPrairie and Benjamin were struggling under their burden of the heavy baskets.

At last, Benjamin said, "Reine, this basket is too heavy. I can't carry it."

Reine looked at him. His face was red in the hot sun. His brown hair was falling in his eyes.

"Okay," she said, "let's rest. I will climb to the top of the hill and have a look. Maybe I will see Papa or Maman coming."

She left them sitting on the ground in the shade of a poplar tree and climbed to the top of her favourite hill. Once there, she climbed onto the top of the spire of sandstone rock that stuck out of the ground like an old rotten tooth. She shaded her eyes from the sun and looked all around. She was startled to see how much of the flat prairie ground the river had covered already. She looked for a way around the gully but where it curved around the bottom of the hill, reddish-brown water was already rushing through it.

Reine felt cold desperate fingers of fear reaching inside her, grabbing her heart, freezing her breath. What if the water kept on rising and rising? Maybe this was another great Flood, like the one Father Gaboury had talked about, when he had come to teach them all their Catechism, so they could become good Catholics.

Maman had been so glad when Father Gaboury had first come to the settlement. "Now, at last, my children," she said, "you can be baptized and received into our good Catholic church."

Reine didn't really know what that meant but if it made her mother so happy, she was glad to do it. Father Gaboury had told them all about God and the angels, and Jesus Christ and the beautiful blessed Virgin Mary. He had taught them to say their prayers and now, every night before they went to sleep, they all gathered around Maman and said their prayers with her.

Perhaps that was what she needed to do right now, say a prayer, she really didn't know what else to do. But she knew she had to be brave and keep on looking brave for the rest of her brothers and sisters. She couldn't let them see how scared she was.

She wondered how she should go about saying this prayer. Was there really a God looking down from the sky to look after all of them, like Maman always said? Her Maman had told Reine many times that God was looking out for all the Lagimodiere family. That was why, Maman said, they had come through so many dangerous times and yet had never been hurt.

If what Maman said was true, then surely God would take a hand, turn back the terrible flood somehow, or help them find a way to a safe place, help them find Maman and Papa, who were probably already looking for them. She knew the farm that Maman had gone to was many miles to the south. Perhaps Maman was already cut off, perhaps she was frantic with fear, wondering about her children.

And Papa had gone far to the north to hunt in the sloughs and marshes of the Lake Winnipeg. He wouldn't even know about the flood until he came home. Often when he went on a hunt, he stayed two or three days.

Suddenly, Reine saw a black dot moving over the prairie. She shaded her eyes again and looked as hard as she could. It was a horse with someone riding. In some places, it was splashing through the water, in some places almost swimming, but it came on and on.

Soon, it got close enough she could see that it was the same rich dark brown as the horse that Dan Archibald rode. Then it got close enough so she could see it was Dan Archibald.

"Dan," she shrieked, stand on the rock and waving. "Dan, we're here, we're over here."

He saw her and waved back. When he came to the muddy ravine full of water, he didn't hesitate. He and his brave horse plunged into the water and came up the other side, the horse snorting and heaving to get itself out and over the mud.

Her feet flew like the wind as Reine ran down the hill to meet him. "Dan," she called. "What is happening? The river... I didn't know what to do, I was so scared."

"Where are the other kids," he gasped, sliding off the horse.

"C'mon," she said. She took his hand and led him through the brush to where the other children were resting. They all leapt to their feet to hug him and crowded around, besieging him with questions.

"What are we going to do?"

"Where are Maman and Papa?"

"Is the river going to flood the whole prairie?"

Reine suddenly realized with embarrassment that she was still holding Dan's hand. She let go and hid her red face by bending down over Pauline and Josette.

"Are you okay?" she asked. "Are you rested? Do you think you can go on?"

"We're fine, Reine," they said.

"I'm fine too," said Benjamin. "This basket isn't that heavy."

"Pauline and Josette, you ride the horse," Dan said. "We'll hang the baskets on the saddle. Then we can move quickly. When we get to the ravine, I'll swim the horse over with you hanging onto the saddle."

"Where is Papa?" said Reine.

"He is still hunting. Someone has ridden to inform the men about the river rising. They'll be coming back as fast as they can. I knew you were home alone because I saw your mother ride by this morning. I came for you as soon as I figured out that you would be cut off by the water."

"Oh thank you, Dan," said Reine. Her knees suddenly felt weak with relief. They loaded the two girls and the baskets on the horse, a basket hanging on each side for balance. LaPrairie and Benjamin ran ahead while Dan and Reine walked silently, side by side, Dan leading the horse.

When they came to the gully, the water looked even higher than it had before.

"How deep is it?" Reine said.

"It's not too bad. The horse can make it," he said. "I'll take Josette and Pauline first, then come back for the rest of you. Then we'll head for the highest ground we can find."

The first trip went well. The horse struggled a bit before reluctantly going into the water. Dan slipped back and held on to the stirrup. They fought their way through the water which foamed and boiled around the horse's legs and belly. Josette and Pauline screamed as the water rose around their legs and soaked their skirts and stockings, but that was it. On the far side, they slid off the horse and then took off their soaked moccasins. Dan unloaded the heavy baskets, then turned the horse around to head back into the water.

But this time the horse had obviously gotten tired of fighting its way through the freezing rushing water. It slipped in the clay gumbo on the side of the ravine. Its legs slipped deep into the mud and to get out it began to rear and plunge. It pulled back hard when Dan still tried lead it into the water. It began to fight and struggle, pulling backwards, the whites of its eyes showing. Dan was down the bank, pulling on the reins, when suddenly his feet slipped on the greasy bank and he slid into the water. His hand let go of the reins. The horse backed away, snorting, then suddenly turned and fled, its tail high in the air, back over the prairie.

Dan was struggling up the greasy bank. slipping and sliding.

Oh no, Reine thought. Now she and her brothers were on one side and Dan was on the other.

"Just wait there," Dan shouted. "I've got an idea." He ran down the bank, picked up a chunk of driftwood, threw it in the water and watched carefully as it floated past Reine and the boys. It lodged on the bank near Reine.

He waded into the water and began to swim, paddling furiously to get across the current. He floated past where Reine was standing but the direction of the current brought him into the bank on their side, as he had foreseen. Frantic, she ran after him, and when he came within reach, she waded into the water and grabbed his hand.

Coughing and choking, he staggered up the bank and sat down abruptly.

"That was too scary," he said. "But we can't wait. The water is still rising. We have got to get over there so we can all stay together. Reine, have you got something you can use as rope?"

She shook her head. Then she thought for a moment.

"Turn your head," she said.

She reached for the bottom of her skirt. It was made of tough homespun wool, woven by one of the Scottish women at Fort Douglas. It was hard to tear but she managed to rip off a strip along the bottom.

"Here," Dan said in her ear. "This will help."

She looked up at him. He was holding out his big hunting knife. She nodded and used the knife to cut off two more long strips. Then she tied them together with her swift strong fingers.

"Okay," Dan said. "Each one of us needs a strong pole and each of us will have to hold on tight to the rope. I've done this before and it works but we have to do it all together."

Dan used his knife to cut them each a strong pole and strip it of leaves and branches.

"Now," he said, "each person will use the pole to balance against the current. You also have to hold onto the rope at the same time, so if you get swept off your feet, we can grab you and get you standing up again. Is everyone ready?"

They nodded.

He led the way into the water. He put Benjamin behind him, then Reine, then LaPrairie. The water quickly deepened until it was boiling around their knees, then their hips, then their waists. Reine fought with all her strength to stay upright. She kept her eyes on her sisters standing on the far bank, their frantic eyes imploring her to make it. The water was so strong. It was like an unseen pair of hands, grabbing at her legs, trying to send her tumbling end over end down the flooded ravine. But she discovered if she leaned hard on her pole, and took tiny shuffling sideways steps, she could keep going. Every step felt like it was going to upend her completely but somehow, it didn't.

Inch by inch, the four of them made it to the far bank, crawled up the slope, and collapsed on the warm prairie grass. They were all shivering and blue with cold, especially Dan. Their clothes were wet through.

"C'mon," Reine said finally. "We've still got to make it to the neighbours, borrow some dry clothes, and find Maman and Papa. C'mon everyone, we will get warm by walking. The sun will warm us too. We have to find out how other people are doing, perhaps someone understands what is going on and where we can go that will be safe."

One by one, they got to their feet. Reine held Josette and Pauline's hands, while Dan strode behind her. He carried one of the baskets and LaPrairie carried the other. They had to splash through other places where the water had begun to spill over the prairie but since these weren't deep or moving too quickly, this wasn't too hard.

At last they came within sight of the next house belonging to the Beauprés. Reine knew as soon as she looked at it that no one was home. It had a strange air of desertion, no dogs barking, no smoke coming out of the chimney, no noise. Reine's heart sank. She had been depending on Monsieur Beauprés to know what to do.

"There's no one here," she said. "We'll have to go on."

"My feet hurt, Reine," said little Pauline.

"Yes, of course they do, my petite, your moccasins are wet and rubbing your feet." Reine said. "Get up on my back and I will be your strong horse."

Reine hesitated.

"Josette, I will be your wild strong horse," Dan said. Reine sighed, relieved that he had understood.

Reine's feet hurt as well, but she knew there was no use complaining. She had to be strong, like Maman and Papa. To keep her mind off her sore feet, she said, "I know what we should do, we can tell stories as we walk along. Remember the stories we heard from Maman and Papa, about all their adventures."

"Yes, yes," chorused Josette and Pauline. "Tell us a story, Reine."

"Well," said Reine, "I can tell you the story of Marie Anne Gaboury. Do you want to hear that story?"

"Yes, yes," everyone cried, even Dan.

"Once there was a beautiful young woman with blue eyes and blond hair, named Marie Anne Gaboury. She lived in Maskinonge, Quebec, on the banks of the Saguenay River. She was so beautiful, all the young men of the village had decided they wanted to marry her but she wouldn't marry any of them, do you know why?"

"Why Reine, why," cried Pauline who had heard this story before but always wanted to hear it again.

"Because she wanted to marry Louis Lagimodiere, but he had gone out west to be a fur trapper and a hunter. So she decided she would wait for him. She became a housekeeper for the priest in the village and all the village people shook their heads. Oh no, they said, what will become of Marie-Anne Gaboury. She will never get a husband. She will never have a family. Poor poor Marie-Anne."

"But then he came back," said Josette. "Tell that part, Reine."

"Yes, he came back. He was tall and strong and he had gained a reputation as a brave trapper and hunter. He had lived with the Indians and learned their language. But he didn't know that Marie-Anne Gaboury had been waiting for him all this time. The night after he returned to the village, there was a big dance. Everybody came. Everybody got dressed up. Marie-Anne wore her prettiest dress, a blue dress that matched her eyes. When she came to the village hall, all the young men wanted to dance with her. But Louis Lagimodiere didn't ask her to dance. He was too afraid because she was so beautiful. So after she had danced with all the other young men, she came over and asked him to dance. Everyone was shocked. A girl asking a man to dance! Imagine! But it worked. They danced together all evening and in a few weeks, Louis asked Marie Anne to marry him. But then he told her he would have to go out west again on another trapping expedition to get some more furs. And do you know what she said?"

"What?" screamed Pauline. She loved this part of the story.

"I'm coming with you, that's what she said. No, no, Louis said. There are bears, and wolves and blizzards and no houses to live in. I'm coming anyway, that's what our mother said. And she did."

"And then what happened?" Pauline asked happily, knowing this part of the story too.

"And then she had us, first me, in a tent on the banks of the Pembina River, and then LaPrairie, whose real name is Jean Baptiste but he is called LaPrairie because he was born on the wild prairie. And then Josette, who was born in the Cypress Hills, then Benjamin, who was born on the Pembina River, like me, and then Pauline who was born in the tent of Chief Peguis, our friend, who took us in when our Papa had to go far away."

"And now Romain," said Josette.

"Yes, now Romain," agreed Reine, "who was born in our beautiful log house which Papa built because Maman said we needed a real home of our own. And now we will grow up here and this will be our land forever and ever."

"Look !" said LaPrairie suddenly. They all turned to look where he pointed. It was the strangest sight any of them had ever seen or could have ever imagined.

A house was floating down the river, bobbing on the current. But the house was on fire. Flames were shooting out of the roof and windows. Over the noise of the river, they could hear the crackling and snapping of the fire. They couldn't take it in. They simply stood, staring.

Then LaPrairie shouted again. "Look, it is Maman, coming for us." He dropped the heavy basket and took off running, bounding over the prairie like a young antelope.

Reine couldn't see anything but she knew her brother had the eyes of a hawk. The Benjamin exclaimed excitedly, "I can hear the wheels squeaking. It is Maman, it is," and he took off after LaPrairie.

"I think I will be very glad to see Maman and the wagon," Reine said carefully. She didn't want to admit to Dan how tired she was.

"I might never straighten up again," Dan admitted grinning. "I think my back will have a big kink in it, just like an old tired horse. Your knees are like little knives in my back, Josette."

"Let's take a break," Reine said, with relief. She and Dan stopped and the two girls slid off their backs.

"Look, there is Maman with the wagon." Reine said. "Quick, girls, run to Maman and tell her we are waiting here resting."

The two girls also took off, squealing with relief at the sight of the familiar cart and their little back pony and their Maman sitting upright, holding Romain in her arms.

Reine and Dan sprawled out side by side on the soft prairie grass. Reine thought perhaps she had never been so tired. Finally, she sat up and peeled off her wet moccasins. Her poor feet were red and covered in blisters. Dan whistled.

"You will need to put some good salve on those," he said. "My mother makes some of the best, she is a good healer."

"Dan, I didn't even thank you!" she said. "You came all that way and helped us so much. What would I have done without you!"

"It was nothing." he said, sitting up as well. His tanned face turned a funny shade of pinky-red. "I was glad to help."

They sat together in silence. Reine's stomach fluttered. This was silly. How could she be nervous around Dan? He was her good friend. But suddenly she couldn't think of a single thing to say. Her mouth had gone strangely dry. She was suddenly conscious of her torn short skirt covered in mud, her hair falling out of its braids and blowing in the prairie breeze, her muddy bare legs.

"I hope Papa will return soon," she said.

"Yes," Dan said. "As soon as you are all safe with your Maman, I will go find my horse and ride to find your Papa and the other hunters. They are probably on their way back by now but they should know what is going on. I have been watching the river and it is still rising. More houses are going to be washed away. I don't understand what is going on, but if this continues, we are going to have to find a place to wait until the water goes down. Maybe we can all go to Bird Hill. We will need food, clothing, blankets. Everyone in the community will need help."

Reine looked at him with admiration. He was like her Papa, a leader, always thinking of other people instead of himself. Papa always said a true leader looked out for everyone else before himself.

"I'd better go meet Maman," she said.

"I will come with you," he said, "and then I will go look for my horse."

He stood up, held out his hand to help Reine. She grasped his hand and he pulled her to her feet. For a moment, they stood side by side. Dan put out his hand and gently wiped the hair out of her eyes.

"You are very brave, Mademoiselle Lagimodiere," he said. "We will all need to be brave, to get through the next few days." He put his hand to his neck and lifted off the beaded necklace that was hanging there. "This will help keep you safe," he said. "My grandmother made it for me."

Slowly Reine took the necklace. She looked at it. It was made of many coloured beads and pieces of bone strung on rawhide. "It's beautiful," she whispered.

Dan took it back and then carefully slipped it over her head.

Sombrely, they turned and trudged over the prairie towards the wagon, towards Maman who was standing now and waving at them, and beyond her, the spreading tossing expanse of brown freezing water, still eating up the prairie.

Chapter Nine

The long line of wagons, animals, settlers walking, dogs, children, straggled up the long hill. People were exhausted. Babies cried, dogs barked, horses whinnied back and forth, cows lowed mournfully. At the head of the procession rode Louis Lagimodiere on his big spotted horse.

"We will camp here on Bird Hill," he said. "There is grass for the animals, water for cooking. Everyday, we will send someone to tell us what the river is doing, and as soon as it goes down, we will go home."

Thankfully, people began fanning out, finding places to put up tents or stretch canvas tarps. Children were sent off to look for firewood, and the cows and horses herded together to graze on the prairie under the watchful eye of several of the younger boys.

Reine climbed down off the wagon and then helped Pauline and Josette to the ground. LaPrairie was one of the boys delegated to guard the herd of horses and cows, and Benjamin was promptly sent off by Maman to gather firewood.

Soon flames blazed up from many fires and the good smell of meat roasting, and vegetables and bannock cooking rose from many campsites.

Reine held Romain and tried to rock him to sleep. He had been so restless and fretful, ever since they had been forced to leave home by the terrible flood. Scouts had come from the camp of Chief Peguis, inviting the Lagimodières to stay with him, but Papa and Maman had decided they would stay with the other settlers. The scouts had told Papa the great flood had been caused by a wall of ice jamming the mouth of the Red River where it flowed into Lake Winnipeg.

Many of the settlers had fled in different directions. Some had even decided to go all the way back to Quebec. Some people had lost everything, their houses, barns, animals and all their belongings had floated away, washed down the river or buried in the thick grey river mud.

The greyish-brown river water was still rolling over their homesteads. It had covered their fields, their barns, and many of their houses. Now they were camped on this small hill, waiting for it to go down.

Every day, Louis Lagimodiere led hunting parties for deer or other game. The men set snares for rabbits and fished the nearby lakes for trout, whitefish and catfish. One day, one of the men brought in a huge sturgeon. When they cleaned the fish and cut it into chunks to distribute to the families they found the fish was full of roe, or eggs.

They mixed the eggs with pemmican to make a rich blend that the women fried in the big heavy black pans over the fire. They ate this along with the oily sturgeon meat. The children had been out all day hunting the grass for wild strawberries and they ate the strawberries combined with creamy milk from the Lagimodiere's cow, which had been found and brought along to the camp.

Reine had been out with her brothers and sisters all day picking wild strawberries. She kept looking for Dan. She knew that he and his family had gone north again with his mother's people but she had thought for sure he would find a way to come and say good-bye. She had heard some of the other people talking. Mr. Archibald was tired of farming, they said, and had decided to go back to trapping fur and hunting buffalo.

Apparently, he had said there was no future in farming and thought people should give up. There had been too many years of discouragement, grasshoppers eating the crops, hot dry winds which came and ate up all the moisture out of the ground, summers with no rain, early frosts each fall, and now the flood had convinced him there was no future in the Red River Valley.

Reine wondered if he was right. Even her mother and father sounded so tired and discouraged.

The group of families that had made it to Bird Hill had all come to a meeting at the Lagimodiere campfire the night before. People gathered around the fire, their children on their knees or sitting on the grass.

Each of them took turns speaking what was in their hearts and minds.

"We have tried so hard," said Monsieur Paquin. "But no matter how hard we work, it seems like the land doesn't want us here. The land is rich and fertile, there is no doubt about that. There is buffalo, fish, berries, so much abundance. But we need more than that. We want to build homes, a community, a church, a school. How can we do that, how can we feel safe if we never know if the river is going to come and eat up all our hard work, or the grasshoppers, or even some Indian tribes who are not our friends and want us to leave?"

Many people nodded at his words. Several other people spoke as well. Some of the newer settlers talked about the long and difficult journey they had made from Scotland to this new land, how they had walked through blizzards, mud, mosquitoes and swamps to get here.

"This is my land now," another said. "We've had a lot of bad luck but it is going to change, I feel it in my bones. I feel like the land is testing us, testing our resolve. It wants people who can match it. It's a vast grand land, and full of beauty. We built our house once, we can do it again." His wife, who was sitting beside him nursing a new baby, nodded, and put her hand on his shoulder. She stood up and looked at the whole circle.

"I stand with my husband," she said. "This baby will have a chance to grow up free, and strong, on our own land. Where we came from in Scotland, we weren't free. We lived our lives at the whim of the landlords, we had no rights there but now we have a chance to make a community, a land, a country of our own where people can live free on their own land. We can fight—we can fight drought and floods and grasshoppers. We'll not be beaten so easily."

Reine waited for her mother or father to speak. Finally, when everyone else in the circle had taken a turn, Marie-Anne Lagimodiere stood up to speak.

"As many of you know," she said, "my husband and I have traveled all over this wild new land. I have borne my babies in tents, in tipis, I have carried them on horseback, on a travois, in wagons and on my back. When they got older, I wanted to come live here and settle down. I want to be somewhere with neighbours, with friends, with a school. Perhaps next year we can build a church for our good Father Gaboury. It is a great sorrow to me that my children have had so little schooling. I have done the best I could, but at least I know their children will have a school, and I look forward to that day.

"And I tell you, my friends," she tossed her head and her blue eyes flashed, "when this flood goes down, I will go home and I will plant my garden and rebuild my home and live with my husband and children in this wonderful place. I know this flood will not come again. I talked to my good friend, Chief Peguis, and he said he had never seen such a flood in his lifetime. He told me it was caused by an accident—the ice jammed the mouth of the river. It might never happen again. I am not going to run away from my home because of a big lump of ice."

When she finished speaking, people looked at each other and nodded. Then Louis Lagimodiere rose to his feet.

"I am not a talker," he said. "I am a hunter, a man of action, not words. I will make sure that every day there is enough food for you and your families until we can go home again. And I will help all I can so each one of us can rebuild our homes. That is my promise."

After that the meeting broke up and people went thoughtfully to the tents and shelters that had been set up.

The next morning, Reine noticed that her father had a secret. He was his usual jovial self in the morning, as they ate their bowls of barley porridge by the fire. But his eyes kept flickering out onto the prairie. He seemed to be waiting for something or someone.

Reine was surprised that he didn't go off hunting or fishing with the other men. She wondered if he was getting sick.

When LaPrairie came in at noon from guarding the horses,

she waited for an opportunity to talk to him alone.

"Is our Papa feeling well?" she asked.

"Of course," said LaPrairie, looking surprised. "Papa never gets sick."

"Then why did he stay in camp today and not go hunting with the men? What is he waiting for? He keeps looking out to the prairie."

"Perhaps he is waiting for word from the scouts about the river."

"But they came back last night," Reine pointed out.

"I don't know," said LaPrairie. "I'll see if any of the other boys know anything."

Late that afternoon, Reine got the answer to her question. She could see a dust trail on the prairie. People were coming on horseback. Papa looked at her and grinned. But Reine could only wait in frustration as the dust cloud came nearer and nearer.

Finally, the people were close enough that she could see they were two of the Cree men from the camp she had visited with Dan. They came up the trail through the brush and dismounted at the Lagimodiere's campfire.

Reine's papa and the men exchanged several quick words in Cree, so fast that Reine couldn't quite hear what they said. But she knew they were talking about the horses.

When the taller Cree man handed the reins of the two horses to Papa, she guessed.

"Papa, you are buying two new horses!" she exclaimed.

"Yes, my daughter," he said laughing. "You and LaPrairie were so brave during the flood that I knew you were ready to take on adult responsibility. And with so many people leaving the settlement, I thought I would grab this opportunity. These are fine horses, bred from the English stock. You may take one to your brother and claim one as your own."

Reine was almost speechless with delight. One of the horses was a beautiful red mare, and the other was a tall black stallion. She stepped forward and stroked the soft skin on the red mare's chest and belly.

"This one," she said.

"Here," Papa said, holding his hands together to make a step for her foot.

He hoisted her easily into the saddle and handed her the reins of the black horse. She guided the red mare back down the hill and out onto the grassy slope where the horse herd was grazing.

All the horses pricked up their ears and began whickering and calling to the newcomers. LaPrairie came running to check on the commotion and stopped in astonishment when he saw Reine.

"For you, my brother," she called. "Look what our Papa has given us."

LaPrairie came slowly forward, walked around the black horse, looked it up and down.

"Mine," he said, as if the reality couldn't quite sink in. Then he added, "I will be a man like my father, a hunter and a leader. Someday, I will have a whole herd of horses, as many as I want."

"C'mon," Reine said impatiently, "Let's go. I'll race you."
Together they galloped out onto the open prairie, side by side

in the hot afternoon sun.

Now, it was a matter of waiting. Day after day, the sun shone out of a cloudless sky, and day after day, the scouts went to check on the river valley. They reported the water was going down, but it was going down very slowly.

Wherever the water had receded, it left a thick skin of gray mud several inches deep all over the grass, the fields, and the bushes.

Finally, after camping on the hill for twenty-two long impatient days, the word came that they had all been waiting for. The river had finally receded back into its bed and left their fields.

The next day was one of apprehension and excitement. What would they find when they went home? Would anything be left?

The Lagimodieres packed up their tent, their blankets, their buffalo robes for sleeping. They packed the two baskets that Reine had saved—and finally they packed Maman's heavy iron.

It took them most of the day to travel back to their homestead. As they came over the last hill, Papa stopped the wagon and they all saw it at once—their beautiful log house was still standing, although the barn, the chicken coop and the fences were all gone.

"Well, that is something to be glad about," said Maman. "At least we will have a roof over our heads tonight. Louis, my dear, I am not sure I want to live in a tent ever again."

For answer, he just grunted and smacked the reins on the

horse's back to start down to the flat land beside the river. As they got closer and closer to their farm, they could see the damage the flood had left. Brush and trees were uprooted and the ground all around their house was covered with mud. The trees by the edge of the river were broken and smashed and the grass lay flat, smothered by the mud.

When they got to the cabin, they were all silent, wondering what they would find inside. They could see from the marks on the walls that the water had come high up the log walls but because the cabin had been built so well, it hadn't floated away like so many other people's houses.

Carrying Romain in her arms, Maman went to the door and pulled it open.

"Phew!" she exclaimed. The inside of the cabin stank of mud and mold. Mud was all over everything, on the floor, on the walls, on their bunks, inside the fireplace.

"It's the vegetables in the root cellar," Papa said. "They've gone rotten. Once we get them out of there, our house will begin to smell better."

"And once we get a fire built in the fireplace and begin to dry everything out, and get this mud scrubbed off the floors and the wall, our house will be a home again." said Maman. "But for now, it looks like we will still be sleeping in a tent."

Papa set up the big canvas tent in the front yard— LaPrairie and Benjamin carried armloads of firewood and built two fires, one in the big clay fireplace inside the house, and one outside on the ground for cooking.

Reine carried two buckets of water from the river, while Josette and Pauline carried the heavy sleeping robes and blan-

110

kets into the tent and made the beds for nightfall. Maman nursed Romain to sleep then lay him on a rug to sleep while she made dinner for all of them.

The next day they worked ferociously hard all day—they kept the fire going in the fireplace to dry out the cabin. Meanwhile, Papa carried the stinking rotten vegetables out of the root cellar and threw them away. Reine, Josette, and their mother scraped the boards and walls clean of the dried sticky mud. The quern, the precious grinding stone, was unharmed but it was also full of mud. Finally, they hung Papa's sword back on the wall, over the fireplace.

Pauline was left to tend Romain, who was now crawling around and trying to get into everything.

When she had a chance, Reine went to look at her bunk. She had left the beautiful beaded moccasins that Mrs. Archibald had given her on the floor under the bunk. She pulled them out. They were soaking wet, blackened and muddy. Reine sank onto the bed, holding them in her hands. She remembered the night she had danced with Dan at the Archibalds' cabin. They had danced every dance together. At the end of the evening, they danced the Handkerchief Dance. When Dan had chased her into the aisle between the clapping, shouting men and women, he had grabbed her, grinned and then gently kissed her on the cheek.

But when it was her turn to chase him, she had been too shy to kiss him. Instead she had ducked her head and run away, to everyone's huge amusement.

By the end of the day, every bone and muscle in Reine's body ached. Her hands burned, her knees and back ached, even her face ached.

"One more day," said Maman with satisfaction. "Then our house will be clean again and we can finally be at home. But we have lost so much," she added sadly. "Clothes, blankets, food, all ruined. I will have to replant the garden. Our chickens are gone. Our barn. Your Papa will have to work so hard to get caught up and ready for next winter."

One more day? Reine thought with dismay. They ate a quick supper and then fell into bed. But the next day brought a surprise as well as hard work. In the afternoon, just as they finished piling the last of their mud-soaked clothes and blankets in a pile to be burned, Monsieur Beauprés rode up on his horse.

"I have a present for you Lagimodieres," he roared. "Something new, something never seen in this land before, something to rid us of the plague of mice and rats."

Carefully holding a basket with a lid, he climbed off his horse. A strange yowling noise was coming from the basket.

They all clustered around him as he carefully took off the lid. Inside crouched a small grey and black striped animal, with a long tail and two big pointed ears.

"A kitten," exclaimed Marie-Anne. "I haven't seen one of these since I left Quebec."

Carefully, she reached out and picked up the tiny, shivering, yowling kitten. She cuddled it under her chin rubbing its soft fur.

"Come, my children," she exclaimed. "Come and say hello to your new friend. I had a kitten when I was a girl. It was called Minou. It used to sleep with me with its little head on the pillow. Oh, what a wonderful present. Thank you, Monsieur Beauprés."

That evening, they moved back into their house.

The fire glowed and snapped in the fireplace—the beds were made, the floor swept, and once more they could gather around the fireplace and listen to Maman and Papa tell stories. The kitten had drunk a bowl of milk and eaten some fish and now it lay curled up and purring in Maman's lap.

Over and over again, they told stories of the flood, of narrow escapes and terrifying moments. Reine and LaPrairie told again of seeing the house on fire floating down the river. Over forty-seven houses had been carried away in the flood. Papa told of seeing a poor dog caught on the roof of a floating house, barking and growling at the water. Many animals had drowned, including cows, horses, sheep and pigs. The wild animals had also been desperate to escape. Snakes, gophers, rabbits, even frogs and toads had covered the prairie, all of them desperately heading for higher ground.

"But so much was saved as well," Papa said. "Someone at Fort Douglas carried sacks of wheat into the belfry of the church. The settlers will not go hungry this year."

Reine slept all that night, a deep dreamless sleep, until she woke in the morning to the sound of Papa calling.

"Come, everyone, come and look," he shouted.

Reine tumbled out of bed in her nightgown. What was going on? What would cause her father to become so excited?

"Come, my children, come," he called again. They ran outside in the chilly gray dawn. It was still early in the morning. The sun was just coming up over the line of prairie in the distance. Reine squinted into the sun, trying to see the black figure of Papa.

"What is going on, Papa?" Reine called. She was frightened. Was the river rising again? Was there some other disaster about to befall them?

Papa walked quickly ahead of them and they all had to hurry to keep up. He led them to the edge of the field he had plowed in the spring and sown with wheat.

"Look," he said. "It is a sign for a future, a sign that God has not forgotten us. We were right to stay, to have faith in our land."

Reine looked past his pointing finger, at the muddy grey ground. Only now it was no longer grey. Instead, it was covered with a shimmering emerald haze.

"It is the wheat," roared Papa with exultation. "The wheat has sprouted and in only three days. It is a miracle. This year will be a good crop, an abundant crop, a crop which will ensure our future."

Maman went to him and put her arms around him. For the moment, the two of them stood there as if there were only the two of them, as if they had forgotten everyone and everything else.

Then Romain, who had been left alone back in his cradle in the cabin wailed, startling Maman.

"Oh goodness me," she said, "my poor little one," and rushed back to the cabin.

Papa also stalked off, followed by LaPrairie and Benjamin.

Pauline and Josette turned and trotted after Maman. "Wait, Maman, wait," called Pauline, and Maman slowed her

114

footsteps, picked up Pauline and took Josette's hand.

Reine was left alone staring at the field of green sprouting wheat.

She fell to her knees and examined the tiny blades, like grass but not grass, wheat which would bring food and life and more settlers to this new country. She was remembering her last meeting with Dan Archibald, who had finally come to Bird Hill to say good-bye, as he had promised.

After he had eaten dinner with Reine's family and talked to Reine's Papa, he asked Reine if she would come with him to hobble his horse for the night. She knew it was only an excuse for them to have some private time but she was so glad to get away from the prying eyes of the camp.

She and Dan collected his horse, and walked away from the camp, to where the other horses and cattle were grazing, tearing grass and chomping it. The night was quiet but it was also full of the sounds of the animals contentedly munching, or an occasional nicker from one of the ponies.

Dan turned his horse loose, then stopped and took her hand.

"You know I am going north again with my family," he said. "My father will take me trapping with him this winter, and we will not return until spring. My father may never return—he is angry with this valley and with the river. But I will come back. I have bought a cart, and next year I will buy another one. I am going to set up a partnership with my friends, hunting buffalo and selling the meat and hides. When I have enough to settle down and buy land, then I will return," he said.

"I will be here," Reine said.

"That is all I need to know," said Dan. Together they turned and walked back to the camp, to the bright flickering fires, the sounds of voices, someone singing, a baby crying, a dog barking, the voices of family and home.

Reine got up and faced the rising sun. She raised her arms in exultation. She was young, she was strong, and the wheat was a promise for the future.

Historical Notes

Reine Lagimodiere was a real person, the daughter of Louis and Marie-Anne Lagimodiere. Marie-Anne Lagimodiere was the first white woman to live in western Canada. She and Louis had eight children and settled on the banks of the Red River, near the town of what eventually became St. Boniface, Manitoba. Reine's sister, Julie, who was not born at the time of this story, became the mother of a very famous Canadian historical figure named Louis Riel.

The flood described in this book happened in 1826 in the Red River Valley. Many settlers and pioneers lost their homes and animals, but after the flood, the wheat did sprout miraculously fast and many settlers had excellent crops that year. This part of Canada is now a famous farming and wheat growing area.

The settlers in the Red River Valley faced many hardships. When grasshoppers ate their crops, they almost starved. They had to learn to cope with blizzards, floods, and wild animals. People of many nationalities and races met and mingled in the Red River Valley settlement. Many settlers were Métis, or as they called themselves, Bois-Brulés. They were of French Canadian and First Nations descent. Other settlers were Scots who had been forced off their land in Scotland by cruel landlords and had come to Canada to start a new life. People spoke French, English, Gaelic, Cree, or a Métis language called Mitchif.

However, for many years, there was a lot of disagreement, anger and some fighting between fur trappers who worked for the NorthWest Trading Company, and the new settlers. The fur trappers believed that farming would ruin the fur trade and put them out of business. Eventually, however, they learned to work together to build a strong community.

In the future, however, there would be another dispute, led by Louis Riel against the Canadian government, over who would own this land.

Glossary

pemmican — a food made from dried buffalo meat, dried berries, and melted buffalo fat

bannock — bread that was made over the campfire

richaud — leftovers fried with potatoes and onions

roobadoo — pemmican, onions and potatoes fried together

quern — two flat stones used for grinding wheat

ox/oxen — a large breed of cattle used for plowing, pulling carts and other farm work

sturgeon — an enormous fish found in many rivers and lakes in Canada

Luanne Armstrong is an award-winning writer, transplanted from the Kootenay region of BC. She has published poetry, adult novels and four previous books for children. She presently lives in Vancouver. She has an MFA from UBC and is now working on a PhD.

Illustrator Robin LeDrew lives near Lumby on a piece of land that she has loved since she was thirteen. She listens to people for a living and writes, draws and paints when she gets the chance. Her illustrated future fantasy *Future So Bright* can be found on the Lumby Community website, www.monashee.com.

If you liked this book...
you might enjoy these other Hodgepog Books:
for grades 5–8

Cross My Heart
by Janet Miller, illustrated by Martin Rose
ISBN 0-9730831-0-7 $8.95

And to read yourself in grades 3–5
or to read to younger kids.

Ben and the Carrot Predicament
by Mar'ce Merrell, illustrated by Barbara Hartmann
ISBN 1-895836-54-9 $4.95

Getting Rid of Mr. Ributus
by Alison Lohans, illustrated by Barbara Hartmann
ISBN 1-895836-53-0 $6.95

A Real Farm Girl
By Susan Ioannou, illustrated by James Rozak
ISBN 1-895836-52-2 $6.95

A Gift for Johnny Know-It-All
by Mary Woodbury, illustrated by Barbara Hartmann
ISBN 1-895836-27-1 $5.95

Mill Creek Kids
by Colleen Heffernan, illustrated by Sonja Zacharias
ISBN 1-895836-40-9 $5.95

Arly & Spike
by Luanne Armstrong, illustrated by Chao Yu
ISBN 1-895836-37-9 $4.95

A Friend for Mr. Granville
by Gillian Richardson, illustrated by Claudette Maclean
ISBN 1-895836-38-7 $5.95

Maggie & Shine
by Luanne Armstrong, illustrated by Dorothy Woodend
ISBN 1-895836-67-0 $6.95

Butterfly Gardens
by Judith Benson, illustrated by Lori McGregor McCrae
ISBN 1-895836-71-9 $5.95

The Duet
by Brenda Silsbe, illustrated by Galan Akin
ISBN 0-9686899-1-4 $5.95

Jeremy's Christmas Wish
by Glen Huser, illustrated by Martin Rose
ISBN 0-9686899-2-2 $5.95

Let's Wrestle
by Lyle Weis, illustrated by Will Milner and Nat Morris
ISBN 0-9686899-4-9 $5.95

A Pocketful of Rocks
by Deb Loughead, illustrated by Avril Woodend
ISBN 0-9686899-7-3 $5.95

Logan's Lake
by Margriet Ruurs, illustrated by Robin LeDrew
ISBN 1-9686899-8-1 $5.95

Papa's Surprises
by Constance Horne, illustrated by Mia Hansen
ISBN 0-9730831-1-5 $6.95

Fuzzy Wuzzy
By Norma Charles, illustrated by Galan Akin
ISBN 0-9730831-2-3 $6.95

And for readers in grade 1-2,
or to read to pre-schoolers

Sebastian's Promise
by Gwen Molnar, illustrated by Kendra McCleskey
ISBN 1-895836-65-4 $4.95

Summer With Sebastian
by Gwen Molnar, illustrated by Kendra McClesky
ISBN 1-895836-39-5 $4.95

The Noise in Grandma's Attic
by Judith Benson, illustrated by Shane Hill
ISBN 1-895836-55-7 $4.95

Pet Fair
by Deb Loughead, illustrated by Lisa Birke
ISBN 0-9686899-3-0 $5.95